When Scales had gone he opened the file and found a copy of the circulated photograph of the missing girl looking up at him. She was beautiful, not pretty, in the first flush of maturity; certain to be the focus of powerful emotions. At first, one had the impression of an open, smiling face but there was something that disturbed him. Her eyes did not smile with her lips; they gave nothing away; they saw, but allowed nothing to be seen.

Was it possible to read so much into a photograph?

It was becoming increasingly likely that this girl had been murdered and Wycliffe believed in the theory of complementarity between killer and victim. Only in mindless killings does a victim play a purely passive role in the drama of death. Almost always there is some action, accomplished or projected, which prompts the killer to strike. So, get to know the victim as a first priority.

D0988026

W.J. Burley lived near Newquay in Cornwall, and was a schoolmaster until he retired to concentrate on his writing. His many Wycliffe books include, most recently, *Wycliffe and the Guild of Nine*. He died in 2002.

By W.J. Burley

Wycliffe and the Three-Toed Pussy
Wycliffe and How To Kill a Cat
Wycliffe and the Guilt Edged Alibi
Wycliffe and Death in a Salubrious Place
Wycliffe and Death in Stanley Street
Wycliffe and the Pea-Green Boat
Wycliffe and the School Bullies
Wycliffe and the Scapegoat
Wycliffe in Paul's Court
Wycliffe's Wild-Goose Chase
Wycliffe and the Beales
Wycliffe and the Four Jacks
Wycliffe and the Quiet Virgin
Wycliffe and the Winsor Blue
Wycliffe and the Tangled Web
Wycliffe and the Cycle of Death
Wycliffe and the Dead Flautist
Wycliffe and the Last Rites
Wycliffe and the Dunes Mystery
Wycliffe and the House of Fear
Wycliffe and the Redhead
Wycliffe and the Guild of Nine

HENRY PYM SERIES
A Taste of Power
Death in Willow Pattern

OTHER NOVELS
The Schoolmaster
The Sixth Day
Charles and Elizabeth
The House of Care

Wycliffe
AND THE
TANGLED WEB

W.J.Burley

An Orion paperback

First published in Great Britain in 1988
by Victor Gollancz Ltd
This paperback edition published in 2001
by Orion Books Ltd,
Orion House, 5 Upper St Martin's Lane,
London WC2H 9EA

An Hachette Livre UK company

A CIP catalogue record for this book
is available from the British Library.

Printed and bound in Great Britain by
Clays Ltd, St Ives plc

The Orion Publishing Group's policy is to use papers that
are natural, renewable and recyclable products and
made from wood grown in sustainable forests. The logging
and manufacturing processes are expected to conform to
the environmental regulations of the country of origin.

www.orionbooks.co.uk

Readers who are acquainted with Cornwall will probably realise that this story is set in Mevagissey, but those who know Mevagissey must forgive major inaccuracies in topography. These are deliberate as I do not want to imply that the people, the events, or the detailed locations described, have any reality outside the pages of this book.

In particular, and fortunately, the Rules and the Clemos, whose troubles are recounted, are families existing only in my imagination.

W.J.B.

Chapter One

The fair girl looked out of place in a doctor's waiting-room; she seemed to glow with health.

The old man thought so; he watched her, his chin resting on arthritic hands clasped over the knob of his walking stick. He watched her steadily, through bleached, expressionless eyes, remembering other girls with honey-coloured skin, speckled with golden hairs; girls with swelling breasts and cheeks that were smooth and soft with the bloom of youth; girls who were old now — or dead.

The woman thought so too. Her immense bulk, confined in a flowered frock, spread over one of the cane chairs; her shopping bags took up another. Her fat, ringed fingers clutched a leather handbag to her abdomen, and she watched the girl through little piggy eyes.

The girl herself seemed unaware of them; she sat in a shaft of sunlight from a high window, idly turning the pages of a magazine. Now and then she glanced at her wrist-watch and at the excluding door of the consulting-room.

The old man said: 'Doctor's on his holidays.'

The girl said: 'Yes.'

'I reckon it takes the locum a bit longer.'

'Yes.'

'Likely he's a bit more conscientious.' The old man laughed, a senile chuckle.

The woman, feeling that the ice had been broken, said: 'You're Rosie Clemo's girl.' It sounded like an accusation.

'Yes.'

'You buried your granny yesterday.'

'Yes.'

'A big funeral. I was there. Lovely lot of flowers too. Sad! 'Course she was coming on. She must've bin eighty? Eighty-one?'

'She was eighty.'

'A happy release in a way, bedridden like she was. I remember Elinor more'n forty year back, teaching in Sunday school. Your poor mother an' me was in her class.'

It meant nothing to Hilda. Although she had been born and brought up with it, village gossip bored her; it was a background, like the chattering of a radio when one's attention is elsewhere. Especially now.

Through the window of the waiting-room she could see the harbour, the light dancing on the water less than a stone's throw away, yet it was another world, a world from which she was cut off.

One of the boats was in, moored against the fish quay — Peter Scoble. He'd been out wreck-netting and she wondered vaguely why he was back so early. He must be running a trip in the afternoon. These thoughts, like the snippets she read in her magazine, drifted on the surface of her mind while underneath there was a great hollowness of apprehension. On the other side of that door, on a slip of paper . . .

The consulting-room door opened and a scrawny little man in a fisherman's jersey came out, clutching a prescription form. He greeted the others briefly and went out.

A pause that seemed unending, then: 'Miss Hilda Clemo, please!' The doctor, a young man with blond curly hair, and wearing a white coat, stood in the doorway.

The girl followed him into his consulting-room and the door closed behind her.

The woman said: 'Snotty little piece, she is!'

The old man said: 'A good-looker though. I dunno where she got it from. Not from the Clemos, that's for sure. And the Rules is no oil paintings.'

The woman followed her own line. 'I know we shouldn' speak ill of the dead but 'er mother was the same, thought she was a cut

8

above the rest of us — an' all they Rules for that matter. I mind when their father kept a shop in Church Street; you'd think 'e done you a favour just by taking your money.'

The old man said: 'I thought Jimmy Clemo would've married again when 'is wife died. I mean, 'e was still a young man an' that girl was no more'n four or five year old.' He started to cough, then pulled out a grubby handkerchief and spat into it. 'Funny! I always thought they Clemos was a warm lot by nature like.'

The woman was deflected. 'There's Esther.'

'Esther!' Surprise set the old man coughing again. 'You don't think . . . God! I'd sooner go to bed with a bag of ol' bones. Anyways she's gone for religion — Catholic, too.' He chuckled. 'Sensible, I s'pose, looking the way she do.'

For a while silence closed in. The old man stared out of the window with unfocused eyes, and the woman stared at the wall with its notices about smoking, about AIDS, and about inoculations against influenza.

The woman said: 'Jimmy Clemo is making a fortune out o' that caravan site. A gold mine, they say.'

'More in it than farming, that's for sure.'

The woman looked at the closed door. 'E's taking 'is time with 'er.'

'Examining 'er, I dare say. I wouldn' mind being that young doctor!'

'You're a dirty ol' man, Willie Prowse!'

At last the door of the consulting-room opened again. Hilda Clemo came through and, without a look, marched through the room and out by the door to the street.

The white-coated young doctor said: 'Mr Prowse, please!'

The quay loungers were parked in a row on one of the seats; tourists and trippers milled aimlessly about, eating ice-creams and wondering what to do with the day. She spotted Ralph Martin farther along the quay, hesitated, decided not to see him, and turned off into one of the alleys before she reached him.

Her slimness made her look taller than she was, and her suntan appeared deeper because of her straw-coloured hair. She wore jeans and a navy-blue, sleeveless, cotton top, moulded to her body; a white logo on the front carried the words: *M.V. Sea Spray*. She walked with the easy, unhurried stride of a young animal in perfect health.

Expectant mother . . . prenatal . . . midwife . . . labour . . . delivery . . . breast feeding . . . Or, abortion. She had brooded on those words and they had disgusted her. The very thought . . .

She turned inland from the harbour, through the square where most of the shops were, and along a narrow street where cottages opened directly on the road. Strangers turned to look at her, women with a certain envy, men with lust. Locals greeted her, but she did not acknowledge them.

She was remembering her sister's pregnancy and the birth of her nephew: Alice's morning sickness and indigestion; her barrel-like figure and unrelieved peevishness. Though in less than six months from the birth, Alice had gone back to leading the life she had led before, with Esther taking charge of the baby . . . A mother by proxy. But what did Alice's life amount to anyway? I'd rather die than end up like Alice!

'Hi!'

A boy she went to school with, studying the same subjects. In less than a year they should be sitting A–levels together. The boy wanted to stop for a gossip but she brushed him off. To be able to think ahead again to A–levels, without the shadow . . .

Almost from the start she had been sure, and in a curious way she had come to terms with it. She had planned exactly what she would do; how she would first break the news to Alice: 'I'm pregnant.' Alice would tell Esther, Esther would have the job of breaking it to her father. She, herself, would tell Ralph Martin; there would be a session with her brother-in-law, Bertie; another with . . .

She was sometimes troubled by the fact that however desperately she wanted to avoid some threatening prospect, a small voice inside her would whisper: 'But if, in spite of everything, it happens . . .' And the voice seemed to suggest something more than resignation.

In those restless nights she had decided that she could predict their reactions, almost the very words they would use.

Beyond the cottages there were larger houses with gardens; then as the ground began to rise, these gave way to fields on one side, and on the other to a screen of trees. She had left the village behind.

Suddenly she realized that she was smiling.

A break in the trees, and she came to a tall, arched entrance with a suspended sign: 'Tregwythen Leisure and Tourist Park. Camping, Caravanning, Golf, Tennis, and Swimming'. From the entrance, a metalled road curved away between grassy slopes, terraced to accommodate the caravans. The vans were well spaced, with trees and shrubs to mitigate their brash intrusion. On one side of the entrance, reached by a short drive, there was a large, stone-built house with a hipped roof and overhanging eaves; the house where she had been born and where she had lived her life so far. On the other side a building in the style of a Swiss chalet carried a sign: 'Reception, Shop and Café. All enquiries.' Beyond the building there were tables for people who preferred to eat out of doors.

Hilda pushed open a door labelled 'Reception'.

Mid-morning is usually a quiet time in any tourist park and her sister, Alice, was making up accounts. Alice's assistant, a lanky girl of Hilda's age, was entering new arrivals from registration slips.

Alice looked up from her ledger. 'Hullo, kid — bored? Never mind, another fortnight and you'll be back at school.'

'Very funny!'

The two sisters were much alike in features and colouring but, at twenty-eight, Alice was already slipping into matronly slackness, beginning to lose her figure and her looks.

Hilda glanced at the girl. 'Can we . . .?'

Alice said: 'Sharon, be a dear and see if you can find that husband of mine; he should be somewhere on the top site. Ask him what happened to the docket for diesel he had delivered on the twelfth.'

The girl took herself off and Alice said: 'That'll keep her out of the way for a bit; Bertie's cutting the grass behind the toilets. Now, kid, what's your problem?'

'I've just come from the doctor.'

'The doctor? You're not ill?'

'No, pregnant.'

She had said it. The words were out.

'Pregnant! Christ!' It took Alice a while to absorb the news. 'Is it definite?'

'Yes.'

'How long?'

'Eight weeks.'

'You must have been pretty sure you'd put your foot in it.'

'I was.'

'Who is it? Ralph?'

'Yes.'

'You're sure?'

'Of course I'm sure! What do you think I am?'

Alice brushed her indignation aside. 'All right, we won't go into that, but don't come the innocent with me, kid! How long has Ralph Martin . . .?'

'It was the first time.'

'You weren't on the pill?'

'No.'

'And he — '

'We didn't intend to go that far.'

'Famous last words.'

'There's no need to be like that.'

'Perhaps not, but I hope you realize Father will go through the roof. What do you want to do?'

'I told the doctor — the locum — that I wanted an abortion but he was difficult.'

'That can be got over. You'll see Hosking when he comes back from holiday.'

It was all going more smoothly than she had foreseen in her

night-time imaginings. Alice was matter-of-fact, prosaic even; so much so that Hilda felt almost cheated.

She was looking out of the window, her back to the office. Across the roadway a young woman sat on the steps of her caravan while her baby, wearing only a nappy, crawled about on the grass. The mother watched with a Mona Lisa smile. Was it conceivable that any woman would actually want to give herself to that?

All the same, she turned back into the room, already growing into the role she had chosen. 'I suppose I could go through with it.' Moving out a pawn.

'And marry Ralph?'

'Yes.'

'The simplest way out — is that it?' Alice was taking her seriously.

'I suppose it could be.'

Alice drew a deep breath. 'Apart from anything else, what would you live on?'

'Ralph is working with his father on the boats.'

'Yes, but Ralph has two brothers, still at school. Charlie Martin manages to make a living for himself and his family but I'd be very surprised if there was enough in it to take on you and the baby. Ralph may want to, and Charlie might agree, but it would mean a thin time all round. For anything more than subsistence you'd be dependent on Father.'

'I'm dependent on him now for everything.'

Alice gave a short laugh. 'You think Father would let you marry Ralph and everything would go on much as it did before?'

'I don't see why not.'

'Then it's time you did. Haven't you noticed how Father looks at you? You're the only one of us who matters: I'm the great disappointment of his life to date; Esther is part of the furniture. As for Bertie . . .'

Alice took a cigarette from a packet on her desk and lit it. 'So it's over to you, kid. As Father sees it, you're going to do brilliantly in your A–levels, then you'll be God's gift to Oxford. A First is a foregone conclusion; then some wonderful job. After that — one day, an acceptable Prince Charming may come along. Of course, for preference, he'll be defective in a vital part of his anatomy.'

Alice exhaled smoke slowly and watched it spiral. 'Do you think he's going to sit back while you put Ralph Martin in place of all that?'

The idea that her father might find her sexually attractive had never occurred to Hilda. It was a new thought, and an intriguing one. For a moment or two it took possession of her mind.

Alice misunderstood her silence. 'Don't worry, kid. It's all in his mind. Men have their fantasies. You happen to be Father's.'

Hilda flicked idly through a little bundle of registration blanks. 'What would you do?'

'About being pregnant? I'd have an abortion. Apart from anything else, seventeen is too young to hand yourself over to a man. You need to learn the not-so-gentle art of self-defence — and I'm not talking about being knocked about physically.'

'Is that what you did before you married Bertie?' She couldn't resist it.

Alice flushed. 'We're not talking about me.'

'Here's Father.'

James Clemo came into the office, his shirt sleeves rolled up, his hands smeared with grease.

'That husband of yours is bloody useless, Alice! The funeral yesterday, half this morning wasted with old Penrose about Granny's will, then I come back here and it's "I can't get the mower to start, Jim!" A ten-year-old boy would be more bloody use! Sometimes I think it's deliberate.'

Alice said: 'Tell him, not me.'

Clemo was stocky, like all the Clemo males before him; his thinning fair hair had a reddish tinge, now tending to grey; his features inclined to fleshiness, and he had a high colour. He went into the toilet cubicle and emerged some minutes later, drying his hands on a paper towel.

He noticed Hilda for the first time. 'Hullo, kid! What are you doing here?'

He looked his younger daughter up and down. 'I don't like you wearing that top thing. It's not . . . not suitable.'

Hilda said nothing.

'I suppose you're going out with the *Spray* again this afternoon?' His manner was hostile, almost threatening.

'Yes.'

Clemo rolled up the paper towel, shied it irritably in the direction of a wastepaper basket, and missed. He turned again to Hilda, obviously about to say something more, but changed his mind. He looked at his wrist-watch.

'Twelve o'clock; the bloody morning gone! See you at lunch, and get that thing off, Hilda; I shall be glad when you're back at school.'

Alice watched him go, then she said: 'See what I mean?'

Hilda told herself: It's like the opening scene of a play.

Hilda walked up the drive to the house and around to the back. Esther was in the kitchen preparing lunch and Alice's little boy, Peter, was building his bricks on the window seat. He looked round as Hilda came in, his solemn blue eyes met hers, but he returned at once to his building.

'Anything I can do?'

'You can lay the table.'

Esther was thirty-six but she looked older; her hair was scraped back into a ragged pony-tail, her thin features were ill-assembled, her pinched little nose was red at the tip and her forehead shone. There were unanswered questions about Esther; she had been adopted as a girl of sixteen by Hilda's grandparents and, from then on, treated as one of the family. Why, no one seemed to know.

Gradually, as she grew into womanhood, Esther had taken over the running of the house and, when Hilda's mother died, it was she who had assumed responsibility for the child's upbringing.

Hilda spread a cloth over the pitch-pine table which occupied the middle of the barn-like kitchen. The Clemos had their meals in the kitchen unless there were guests. Though much of their

15

land was rented off, they followed the traditions of their farming ancestry; their house had the appearance of a farmhouse and their ways were the ways of a prosperous farming family.

'What's the matter with you?' Esther spoke over her shoulder. She was straining boiled potatoes at the sink.

'Me? Nothing.'

Esther tipped the potatoes into a dish and slid the dish into the grill compartment to keep warm. 'There's something, my girl, and you might as well tell me first as last.'

It was true that, through the years, Hilda had confided more in Esther than in anyone else, but the idea that she was incapable of keeping a secret from her was one of Esther's illusions.

Six places: knives, forks, spoons, side-plates . . . a special place for Peter: a high cushion, and his own cutlery; his Snoopy mug instead of a glass. Hilda worked mechanically, savouring the thought that by the evening they would all be trying in their different ways to adjust to the idea of her pregnancy.

It was interesting.

'No need to take it out on the china, whatever it is! You've been behaving very queer lately, Hilda, and it's getting worse.' Esther broke off. 'Here's Bertie so we'll talk later.'

Bertie was an obvious intruder into the Clemo clan, dark with sallow skin, and black hair which he allowed to grow long at the back. 'My daughter's married a wog!' — Clemo's comment on his son-in-law.

'Has anyone seen Alice?'

Nobody answered, and Bertie joined his son by the window. 'If you put that one there . . .'

Peter's voice came, shrill: 'No, Daddy! Don't do it; I want to!'

Esther laughed.

James Clemo was eating his meal with scarcely any idea of what was passing his lips. He was uneasy, uncomfortably aware that something was going on behind his back. Was it his fancy? If so, why had the notion come upon him with such force? It had started when he came across Hilda in Reception . . .

Esther had her antennae out too; he could tell by the way she darted glances around the table that he wasn't the only one to sense — to *know*, that something was up.

Alice, too. Out of character, she was trying to make conversation: 'I keep feeling I ought to go upstairs to Granny; it's hard to realize she's gone . . .'

They kept things from him and schemed behind his back, though it was he who gave them the chance to make a decent living. It was his management which kept the act together, and what did he get from any of them?

His gaze fell on Bertie. Bertie — what in hell had persuaded Alice to marry him? Too clever by half — and cunning; you never knew where you were with him. Well, this morning he'd had to listen to a few home truths. But there was no satisfaction in bawling him out, he never answered back. You couldn't have a bloody good row, he just looked at you . . . supercilious. No bite and yet not to be trusted. Did Alice know how little he was to be trusted? Anyway it served her right.

Mother is dead — of old age. That's a stage in a man's life. I'm getting old myself; knocking fifty. And what have I got to look forward to?

Hilda.

His expression softened. The kid seemed very subdued, thoughtful; she scarcely looked up from her plate though she was not eating much. Still wearing that damned sleeveless thing — might as well be topless; defying him. Sex! Youngsters these days are pickled in it from the cradle and it hits them hardest when they most need to concentrate on other things. A–levels in less than a year. He worried about Hilda; too boxed up. He'd no idea what went on in her head. No mother, but how the hell could he be expected to . . .? Alice could do more. Hilda was seeing too much of the Martin boy — probably innocent enough, but you couldn't be sure. He'd have a word with Charlie . . .

That bastard, Bertie, was eyeing Hilda on the sly . . . He wondered if the girl had any idea of the dynamite around her.

Christ! I'm getting morbid!

Saturday afternoon

By two o'clock Hilda was on the quay. *Sea Spray* was berthed by the steps. Charlie Martin, Ralph's father, was there.

'Going out with the boy?'

The words were plain enough but their implication was as vague as his half-smile.

'Yes.'

Charlie Martin was a huge man, shaped like a barrel. A thick, dark moustache just failed to hide his prominent lips and he had little, bright eyes which often said more than his words.

'Father all right?'

'Yes, thank you, Mr Martin.' Faced with Ralph's father she felt uneasy.

'Ralph's down in the launch.'

A board at the top of the steps carried a chalked notice: 'M.V. Sea Spray. 3½ hour cruise. Dodman and Caerhays. Landing at Gorran Haven for Cornish Cream Tea. Leave at 2.15. Tickets from the Boat Office.'

Hilda started down the steps. The *Spray* was a beamy launch, a good sea boat but on the slow side. The engine ticked over; Ralph was aboard, arranging cushions for the comfort of tender bottoms. He looked up, saw her, and no words were needed. 'I didn't know if you'd come . . .'

Ralph was nineteen, five-feet ten and sturdily built. His hair and eyes were dark; the Martins were said to have Spanish blood. Most of the girls in the village were after him but he had eyes only for Hilda. Perhaps she should have felt flattered.

Only a slight, oily swell disturbed the surface of the harbour, just enough to sway the masts of the moored craft, but outside white crests glistened in the sun.

Hilda looked up at the sky. 'What is it? Sou'west?'

'Just about. They'll have a bit of chop going and an easy ride back. They like it that way — gives their teas a chance to settle. We'll do the Dodman and Caerhays on the way out and put in at the Haven fourish.'

The passengers were arriving: middle-aged couples, spinster school teachers in pairs, and some elderly folk who had to be helped aboard. These afternoon cruises were losing out to fishing trips: 'No experience required; all gear provided'. Ralph and his father made three such trips a day in good weather, and this cruise of Ralph's was known as 'the ambulance run'.

At two-fifteen Hilda cast off and Ralph took the launch through the maze of moored craft and out between the heads. Once in the open sea he handed over to Hilda and went aft to chat up his passengers. There was more interest in the girl than in the coastline.

'Is she your sister?'

'No, a friend.'

Beyond Chapel Point they were heading into the wind and the old boat lived up to her name, slapping sheets of spray over the wheelhouse to fall on the passengers. Ralph issued them with plastic cover-alls and found a seaman's jersey for Hilda. She put it on and he joined her at the wheel.

It was from that moment the trip assumed an importance wholly unsuspected by anyone aboard. The young couple stood, side by side, swaying to the motion, the girl's hands rested lightly on the wheel, keeping bow to the sea, so that they rode easily with scarcely any roll. It was obvious that the two were engaged in earnest conversation but nothing could be heard above the hiss of the water and the steady beat of the motor.

A mile or so beyond Chapel Point they were running between a line of vicious-looking rocks and the shore. Two shags, their wings spread in heraldic posture, sunned themselves on adjacent pinnacles, coaxing out cameras and binoculars from under the plastic sheets.

Ralph turned to his passengers. 'The Gwineas Rocks.' He pointed. 'See the bell buoy? And listen . . .'

They listened, and heard the slow, rhythmic clang of the bell, rocked by the waves. Coming across a waste of sea it is one of the most haunting sounds known to man.

'We'll take a closer look coming back.'

A promise never kept.

'The village you can see on the shore is Gorran Haven and that's where we shall put in for tea later. The church on the hill is Gorran church. It's been a day-mark for centuries . . .'

Days later Miss Jessup, a schoolteacher from Essex, precise and well preserved, would be asked: 'When did you first observe the young couple to be quarrelling?'

Miss Jessup would purse her lips and quibble over the words: 'I wouldn't say they were quarrelling; it seemed more of a disagreement.'

'And you first noticed they were disagreeing — when?'

'About the time we were passing those rocks, after the boy told us about the bell.'

'Yes, anybody could see they were having an argument. I said as much to the wife and she said "a lovers' tiff". The wife is romantic.' Mr Alec Shipman, a retired builder from Preston.

On the other side of the Dodman they caught the full force of a stiff south-westerly and there were signs of nervousness; the old launch smacked into the occasional rogue wave and rebounded with a jolt; the engine stuttered, then resumed its normal beat. A glimpse of Caerhays Castle seemed to calm all fears; the Nash façade, a Disney castle, peering through trees and fronting the shore. It set the cameras clicking; they went in close and waved to people on the beach.

A broad sweep, and they doubled back. With a following sea it seemed much calmer. As they approached Gorran Haven on the return trip Ralph took the wheel and brought the launch into the little harbour. It was while he was edging alongside that Hilda suddenly jumped the gap and ran up the steps.

At the top she peeled off the jersey he had loaned her and dropped it into the boat. She called back: 'I'm catching the bus home.'

By the time Ralph had berthed she was striding between the holiday-makers on the beach and he still had his passengers to put ashore.

'I felt sorry for the boy — the look on his face!' Mr Shipman, the builder.

Ralph said: 'The café is up on the right; you can't miss it. Just show your boat tickets. We've got an hour.'

The *Sea Spray* was late back and Ralph's father was waiting at the

top of the steps. When the passengers were ashore he said:
'Trouble?'

'Choked feed.'

'Where's Hilda?'

'She's coming back by bus.'

Charlie looked at his son but made no comment.

Chapter Two

Saturday evening

It was left to Esther to break the news of Hilda's pregnancy to her father and he took it badly. He looked bleak and helpless, with none of his usual bluster.

'Why wasn't I told?' Plaintive, rather than aggressive.

He was in the old farm office, next to the kitchen, seated at a roll-topped desk which had belonged to his father and grandfather before him.

Esther was brusque. 'I'm telling you now. Hilda only knew herself this morning; she told Alice just before lunch, and Alice told me this evening.'

'Why didn't Hilda come to me?'

'Would you expect her to?'

'Where is she now?'

'She's not back yet.'

Sitting at his desk, his red face creased in concern, his flimsy half-glasses perched on the end of his nose, he looked both pathetic and slightly ridiculous.

'She should have been in an hour ago.'

'Hilda left the party when they put into the Haven for tea. It seems she had a difference with Ralph and walked out on him.'

Clemo nodded. 'That shows she's still got some sense. I suppose that bloody boy is the father?'

'Yes.'

'I'll break every bone in his body.' But he said it mechanically, without conviction.

'She told Ralph she was catching the bus home but there's only one bus and that got in not long after the *Spray*.'

A new thought occurred to him, triggering fear: 'You don't think she'd do anything daft?'

'Not Hilda. She was talking to Alice quite sensibly about an abortion.'

'Abortion!' The word distressed him.

He reached for the telephone.

'What are you going to do?'

'Phone the police.'

Esther was caustic. 'What will you tell them? "My seventeen-year-old daughter hasn't come home and it's a quarter past seven."'

He glared at her angrily but he did not lift the telephone. 'You're enjoying this!'

'Think what you like.'

He passed a hand over his forehead. 'There's a girl — a school-friend she sometimes spends a weekend with, lives in the Haven . . .'

'Paula Simmonds — yes, you could try.' She leafed through the phone book. 'Here you are; the number is four-two-four-five-three-four. But don't make a fool of yourself. Hilda has probably gone some place where she can think things out.'

He grabbed the telephone and began to dial but fumbled it. 'Here! You do it.'

The usual ritual, then: 'Mrs Simmonds?'

A brief exchange, and Esther replaced the telephone. 'They haven't seen her. In any case Paula is in London, staying with relatives.' She added after a pause: 'If she walked home over the fields I suppose she could have called in at Tregelles.'

Clemo looked doubtful. 'You think she might? Phone and ask — I can't.'

'But you think I can.' Esther was mildly contemptuous but she looked up the number, dialled, and waited. They could hear the rhythmic burr, then a harsh voice said: 'Tregelles Farm.'

'Aunt Jane? It's Esther . . . Hilda was supposed to have been

23

walking home from the Haven across the fields and she hasn't turned up. James is worried . . .'

The voice cut across her words: 'I haven't seen her, if that's what you want to know. I've got trouble enough with your Auntie Agnes wandering off whenever I take my eyes off her. I can't watch her day and night. Anyway, I haven't seen Hilda.' The line went dead as she replaced her telephone.

James said: 'Bitch!' He stood up. 'I'm going to look for her.'

'You'd do better to stay here by the telephone if you're that worried. Alice and Bertie and I will do it. Bertie can cover the lanes in the car and Alice and I will walk the footpaths before dark.'

Clemo hesitated, then gave in. 'You think I'm making a fuss but I'm worried about the girl, Esther.'

Esther shrugged. 'Hilda isn't the sort to come to much harm; she knows how to look after herself.'

'She could be frightened to come home.'

'Frightened? Of you? You must be joking!'

By eleven o'clock, and still with no news, James would be put off no longer; he telephoned the police.

Because so few stations are manned at night he found himself talking to subdivision. A world away from the days when you phoned your local bobby, probably called him by his first name — or you spoke to his wife.

'How old is your daughter, sir?'

'Seventeen.' He said it apologetically. Blast Esther!

'Eleven isn't very late for a young woman to be out these days, sir. Do you have any particular reason for concern?'

It was too much. James bellowed: 'Yes, I do have a particular reason!' But he calmed down at once. 'Sorry! I'm a bit on edge.'

A couple of minutes more of the same and the upshot was that they would send a patrol car. 'Within the next half-hour, sir. Give the officer all the details . . . But I shouldn't get too concerned. In the vast majority of instances there is a perfectly simple explanation.'

Clemo waited on his doorstep. The night was very still and clear. He could see the lights of the village and, beyond, the faintly luminous sea. A couple of caravanners' cars drove into the site but caravanners generally are early to bed and most of the vans were in darkness. In a few of the tents on the high level, lamps glowed dimly through blue and green and orange canvas. It seemed long but, in fact, it was less than twenty minutes before he saw the blue lights of a police patrol car turning off the road.

One of the two-man crew stayed on radio watch while the other followed Clemo into the drawing-room, a large room, rarely used, and smelling of damp. Alice joined them.

'Constable Baxter — now, sir, about your daughter . . .'

Clemo told his story and the policeman listened; an old hand who had been in the force long enough for the greed and lust and frailty of humans to be all in the day's work. An unmarried girl of seventeen, pregnant — pooh!

'This young man — Ralph Martin — have you spoken to him, sir?'

'I have,' from Alice. 'He's very worried; he's been out on his bike all the evening looking for her.'

'Did he say what they'd quarrelled about?'

'He was upset because Hilda told him she was going to have an abortion. He wanted them to marry and have the baby.'

Constable Baxter made notes. Police notebooks must be a virtually untapped source in the field of literature.

'So there was no question of him denying responsibility?'

Clemo said: 'He's no bloody option! My daughter is a decent girl.'

'Of course, sir! Anyway I shall talk to the lad, but it's as well to have the background clear. The boat put in at the Haven for the passengers to have tea and your daughter left, saying that she would come home by bus.'

'Which she didn't!' Clemo made the point with emphasis. 'I hope you realize you're only getting one side of the story — his.'

'For the moment it's all we can get, but don't worry, young Martin will be questioned and we're not fools.'

'How about searching for her?'

The policeman looked out of the window into the darkness. 'What would be the use, sir? If she still isn't home by first light we shall get busy quick enough. Incidentally, if she was walking home from the Haven, which way would you have expected her to come?'

It was Alice who answered: 'It depends. If she wanted the walk to think things out, she might have come by the coast path, but that's a long way round. The quickest is the field path through Tregelles, my aunt's farm, which adjoins our land just up the valley.'

'Tregelles.' Did the policeman's repetition of the name carry a certain inflection? 'You've been in touch with your aunt?'

'Yes, but she hasn't seen Hilda. During the evening two of us walked the footpaths she might have used and my husband has driven over the lanes.'

The policeman nodded. 'You've done all you could; try not to worry. In the morning we'll start an organized search — if necessary. We'll question people in the Haven who might have seen her; we'll talk to passengers on the trip who might have overheard something, and we'll put out a request for information on the local radio. Of course the coastguard will be alerted and all our officers . . .

'Now, sir, madam, I want a description of Hilda and of the clothes she was wearing, then a recent photograph.'

The black marble clock on the mantelpiece chimed the quarter: a quarter past midnight.

Charlie Martin and his family lived in a little square house set above the level of the harbour. When the police rang his doorbell it was Charlie who threw up the sash of an upstair window.

'What's up?'

'Police.'

'I can see that. What do you want?'

'A word with your son, Ralph.'

No argument. A minute or two later Constable Baxter was admitted to the front room by Charlie who had pulled on a pair of trousers over his pyjamas.

26

'The boy will be down in a minute; he's dead-beat.'

Charlie trusted his bulk to a protesting cane chair.

'Of course it's about the girl. He wanted to stay out all night looking for her but I wouldn't have that. Waste of time!'

Ralph came in looking drawn and tired. He perched himself on a chair next to his father.

'Just one or two questions. You quarrelled with Hilda this afternoon during your boat trip?'

'It was my fault; I was a fool.' His voice was unsteady.

Charlie said: 'Nothing of the kind! The boy didn't want his child — my grandchild — put down like an unwanted kitten.'

'I should have waited until Hilda had had a chance to think things over; it was no place to start talking about it with all those people looking on.'

The walls of the little room were almost covered with framed photographs, the subjects about equally divided between boats and members of the family. Pride of place went to an enlargement of a couple who could only have been Charlie's parents.

'Your quarrel became heated?'

'No, it didn't — '

'Tell me about it.'

The boy told.

'And when you put in to the Haven, Hilda left?'

'Yes.'

'Had she said that was what she was going to do?'

'No! I'd no idea — she was up the steps and away before I berthed and she just said: "I'm going home by bus." I couldn't understand it; I mean, we hadn't really quarrelled — just argued a bit.'

Constable Baxter looked the boy in the eyes. 'And that was the last time you saw her?'

'Yes. By the time I'd tied up and got the passengers off she was nowhere to be seen.'

'When did you first have any idea that Hilda might be pregnant?'

'This afternoon, when she told me.'

'You had no suspicion before then?'

'No.'

'But you must have known that what you were doing might lead to just that.'

Ralph coloured, looked at his father and away again. 'I didn't realize that what happened . . . I mean, I didn't think it could be, well . . . so easy.'

Sunday morning

By Sunday morning there was still no news of the missing girl. Her description had been circulated, the coastguard alerted and, at ten o'clock, the local radio broadcast an appeal for information. In addition, police and volunteers with dogs searched the lanes and footpaths, the hedges and ditches, over the whole neighbourhood. Police made random calls on householders in the hope of gleaning something.

Several people in the Haven knew the girl as a friend of Paula Simmonds, and three of them had seen her on Saturday afternoon. All three agreed that she had been hurrying away from the harbour, alone. This was consistent with her either catching a bus or walking home. The bus driver, questioned, said that he had picked up four passengers in the village, none of them in the least resembling Hilda Clemo.

The inquiry had been upgraded. If the girl (in law, a 'young person' — turned fourteen but not yet eighteen) was later found in a ditch, raped and strangled, officialdom had no wish to be accused of having dragged its feet. But the dilemma is real; the police must think twice before starting a massive hunt for every teenager who chooses to strike out for the bright lights without telling the family. But the feeling was growing that here was something different.

Station staff, bus drivers and taxi drivers at Truro and St Austell were questioned. But did the girl have any money with her? She had been carrying a shoulder-bag but nobody knew what was in it. The whole thing was made more difficult because it was Sunday.

Judicious telephoning discovered the whereabouts of some of *Sea Spray*'s passengers. It happened that three of them were staying at the same hotel.

The three were: Miss Jessup, the schoolteacher, and Mr and Mrs Alec Shipman, the retired builder and his wife. They added a little to the sum of police knowledge. Nobody had thought to enquire what Ralph Martin did while his passengers were having their tea. The three disclosed that he had not stayed with his boat; they thought he had gone after the girl.

'Did he go after her at once?'

'No, he couldn't do that; he had to tie up and see us ashore.' Mr Shipman.

'He passed me, almost running, just as I was entering the café.' Miss Jessup. 'And he didn't get back to the boat until some time after we were due to leave.'

'How long after?'

'Well, we were given an hour and we must have been waiting at least another twenty minutes.'

Mrs Shipman agreed. 'All of that. And he wasn't there to help the old people back on the boat. When he did arrive he was panting like he'd been running.' She added, after a pause: 'I must admit I felt sorry for the lad, he looked as though he'd been crying.'

'And when we did get away we went like the clappers.' Mr Shipman with a self-conscious laugh.

On Sunday afternoon Ralph Martin was 'invited' to the subdivisional police station to make a statement. He was taken in a police car. He sat in a gloomy little room with a high window, and a uniformed sergeant who looked like an undertaker wrote out what he said on a form. At the head of the form a declaration, which he was asked to sign, agreed he was making the statement voluntarily, and was aware that what he said might be used in evidence. His hand trembled so much that he could scarcely control the pen.

He was scared but all went smoothly until he came to the bit where Hilda left the boat as he was berthing at the Haven.

'When your passengers were ashore did you stay with the boat?'

Hesitation, then: 'No.'

'What did you do?'

'I went after Hilda, trying to catch her up.'

'Why?'

'I wanted to say that I was sorry for upsetting her.' He blushed.

The sergeant wrote: 'I wanted to say that I was sorry.' It seemed absurd, written down like that. Had the grim faced sergeant ever chased a girl to say that he was sorry?

'Did you find her?'

'No.'

'How far did you go?'

'I went to the bus stop but she wasn't there. I thought she might have decided to walk so I went along the coast path a little way — '

'But you didn't find her?'

'No, I didn't.'

'I did not find her' was written on the form.

'Why didn't you tell the officer who questioned you last night that you followed the girl?'

A moment of confusion. 'I didn't want Father to know.'

'That you'd followed her?'

'That I'd left the launch, that I was late getting back with the passengers waiting, and them getting aboard without me being there. I mean, there's insurance, and all that.'

'I did not mention this because I did not want my father to know . . .' It was written down with the rest.

Monday morning

On Monday morning a report on the investigation appeared in the weekend file of incidents on the desk of detective Chief Superintendent Wycliffe, at police headquarters. Somewhere along the line a note had been appended. 'There are aspects of this incident which give reason for concern.' Somebody protecting his rear.

Wycliffe told his personal assistant, the unflappable Diane: 'Find out what this is supposed to mean and what they're doing about it.'

The answer came within half an hour. 'The DI is querying possible homicide. The girl is from a stable background and though she's pregnant it's thought unlikely that she would do anything dramatic.'

'Then why couldn't he say so?'

'They're pursuing enquiries.'

'Yes, and I know what that means. What does he think I am? A reporter?'

Diane maintained a discreet silence.

'Ask Mr Scales to come in.'

Diane went out with the haul from the morning's paper-chase. She would hint to John Scales that sir's mood was unpredictable and the word would filter down through the hierarchy. Then an unsolicited cup of strong black coffee.

All because a perfect Sunday, weather-wise, had been frittered away on uninvited guests: 'I hope you don't mind us dropping in like this but it's been such ages . . .'

It was some time before John Scales arrived. He was Wycliffe's deputy, a good administrator who looked more like a bank manager than a policeman. He brought a slim file of reports on the incident so far.

'I've also been in touch by phone. It amounts to this, sir: they seem to have done all that could be done in the way of organised search, using volunteers under supervision. They've covered the ground, including unoccupied buildings, with special attention to the shortest route the girl might have taken. I can show you on the map . . .'

Scales spread a large-scale Ordnance map on the desk. 'Here's the field path; it runs through fields belonging to Tregelles Farm which adjoins the Clemo caravan site and belongs to a relative. Here, where the path enters Clemo land, it passes through woodland and skirts a disused quarry which is flooded. At the moment they've got a frogman making an underwater search there.'

There was a pause while Wycliffe brooded over the map, then Scales went on: 'The local boys are doing pretty well.'

'Perhaps, but I think it's time we took over, John. Get a small team together — Kersey in charge.'

They discussed availability, who was free or could be freed. Balancing one against the other with the fact of leave. Then there was the question of a base.

'A mobile Incident Van to start with, John, and see how we get on.'

Rank allowed Wycliffe to stand aside from *i*-dotting and *t*-crossing. Delegation is the magic word but it had taken him a long time to learn it.

When Scales had gone he opened the file and found a copy of the circulated photograph of the missing girl looking up at him. She was beautiful, not pretty, in the first flush of maturity; certain to be the focus of powerful emotions. At first, one had the impression of an open, smiling face but there was something that disturbed him. Her eyes did not smile with her lips; they gave nothing away; they saw, but allowed nothing to be seen.

Was it possible to read so much into a photograph?

It was becoming increasingly likely that this girl had been murdered and Wycliffe believed in the theory of complementarity between killer and victim. Only in mindless killings does a victim play a purely passive role in the drama of death. Almost always there is some action, accomplished or projected, which prompts the killer to strike. So, get to know the victim as a first priority.

But Wycliffe thought that this girl might prove very difficult to know.

He was late arriving at his usual restaurant for lunch and as he made his way to his favourite table he exchanged nods with other regulars already assembled.

Teague's Eating House, established 1892, had changed little in nearly a century. A long, narrow room like a railway coach, with booths down one side. No music, very little conversation; even the waitresses responded to discreet signals rather than to the spoken word. There he could brood.

'The lamb, today, sir . . .'

A half-pint of Stella Artois, nicely chilled, was placed to his hand. By the time he had drunk this his lamb was ready. No dessert, but a large cup of black coffee.

He paid at the cash desk by the door where a wizened little man put his bill on a spike and transacted money from an open drawer.

'Good day, Mr Wycliffe!'

It had a reassuring air of permanence.

Back at the office he glanced through the memos on his desk. One concerned the missing girl: 'Hilda Clemo: Missing person inquiry. Underwater search of quarry — result negative.' Bloody jargon! Why couldn't they say: 'We didn't find her.' He was irritable and impatient.

'Proposals for the Reorganisation of Night Patrols with special attention to Co-ordination between Crime and Traffic.' A ten- or twelve-page memorandum from the chief's office for circulation to senior staff with a note: 'Comments, please.'

He took a scribbling pad and opened the memorandum at page one: Objectives, numbered one to seven. He stared at the page and passed the next few minutes manicuring his nails with a match stick.

It was a quiet time; serious crime was in temporary recession while the professionals relaxed in the Seychelles or the Bahamas. For a fortnight the sun had shone conscientiously from rising to setting while people watered their gardens and disported themselves in swimming pools, so that the water boards believed themselves conspired against by God and man.

Half the population seemed to be on holiday and Wycliffe kept office hours, doing office work, cosseted and confined in his soundproofed, air-conditioned cell. At five he would deal with his outgoing mail, by six he would be home.

Somehow a blowfly had pioneered the maze of corridors to reach his office and was buzzing, fruitlessly, against the window which was sealed. For a while Wycliffe pursued it, without success, then accepted a truce and returned to his chair. The fly came to settle on his papers.

He reached his decision when his clock showed three minutes past three. A brief tidying operation, a couple of telephone calls, and he confronted Diane in her office.

'I'm going down to see how Kersey is getting on.'

'Now?'

'Now.'

'But what about — '

'I shall be home this evening and here in the morning.' He felt like a schoolboy, a little puffed up by his bravado.

When he arrived in the village the tourists were beginning to drift back to their hotels, their boarding houses, self-catering apartments and camp sites. Most of the day-trippers had already gone home. He found the Incident Van already parked at the western end of the wharf, near the fish quay. Somebody had been busy.

Dixon was duty officer and Kersey was in the larger cubicle being briefed by Detective Inspector Rowse from division. Rowse was young, new to his rank, climbing the ladder and determined not to lose his footing.

Wycliffe cross-questioned him about the inquiry. 'Obviously you've come close to deciding that the girl is dead and that we've probably got a homicide on our hands.'

'It looks that way, sir.'

'In which case we are looking for a body. I gather you've searched the area pretty thoroughly and that you've put frogmen into this quarry. Is there any possibility that the body might have been dumped in the sea?'

Rowse frowned. 'It's not easy to dispose of a body from the shore, sir.'

'I realize that; you need a boat. Is that a problem around here?'

Rowse was cautious, unsure of the extent to which this was a test. 'You have to get the body to the boat, sir, and unless you're a boatman you've got a job to do much along the waterfront here, day or night, without being closely watched. Anyway, as I've just been telling Mr Kersey, a recent development makes the whole idea unlikely. It looks as though the girl was on her way home, by way of the field path through the farm shortly after half-past four on Saturday afternoon.'

'Let's hear it.'

'Just before I left the office on my way here, I had a telephone call from a Mrs Rushton. She lives on the outskirts of Gorran and she says that on Saturday afternoon, at about half-past four, she saw a young man and a girl on the stile near her house. They seemed to be arguing and she had the impression that the young man was very upset. From her descriptions it seems certain that she saw Hilda Clemo and Ralph Martin.'

'But Martin denied seeing the girl after she went ashore.'

'Which makes him a liar.'

Rowse had a positive manner which did not impress Wycliffe who was seldom positive about anything.

'Why didn't your witness come forward earlier?'

'She's an elderly woman, living alone; she'd heard about the missing girl but didn't connect it with the couple she saw until, talking to a neighbour this lunch-time, she mentioned the incident and was persuaded to report it.'

It was all eminently reasonable.

Wycliffe turned to Kersey. 'We'd better send someone to take her statement.'

'I've already done that, sir.' From Rowse.

Wycliffe stared at the young man with a steady expressionless gaze, oddly intimidating. 'I assume you haven't arrested the boy?'

Rowse looked puzzled. 'No, sir. Surely the next step would be to have him in for further questioning?'

'Yes. Well, this stile where the young couple were having their argument, where exactly does it lead?'

'To the footpath across the fields through Tregelles, which is farmed by relatives of the Clemos, past the quarry, and on to the caravan park.'

'Tell me about the girl's family.'

'Her father, James Clemo, is a widower, his wife died when Hilda was four.'

'Married again?'

'No, sir. Then there's Hilda's sister, Alice: twenty-eight or nine, married to Albert Harvey — Bertie to the family. They have a little boy and they live in the house with father and work in the caravan park. A relative, Esther Clemo, looks after the house.

'That's the lot, sir, but perhaps I should mention that James Clemo's mother died last week and was buried on Friday. That is to say the day before Hilda went missing.'

Wycliffe nodded. 'That's clear enough. Now about the people at the farm — Tregelles. You've talked to them, I suppose?'

'Yes, sir, of course. They're called Rule: a widow in her sixties and her son; they're related to the Clemos through Clemo's mother, the old lady who died last week. The son is weak in the head but he seems to manage most of the farm work, though I gather they don't do a lot of real farming; mainly they take in other people's livestock for fattening. There's also an old woman who lives with them, Mrs Rule's sister-in-law.'

'What are they like?'

'The son seems harmless, amiable, and according to the local man he's never been in any trouble. His mother tends to be aggressive. I didn't see the old lady but I gather she's senile. They deny having seen the Clemo girl on Saturday but I got the impression they were holding something back.'

'Any idea what it could be?'

'No, sir, but I intended to look into it if I stayed on the case.'

'I see. Well, as things are, if you've finished handing over to Mr Kersey I expect you'll be anxious to get back to your own desk.'

Rowse left, wondering which foot he had put wrong — and where.

Kersey said: 'He's done very well. You were a bit rough on him, don't you think, sir?'

Wycliffe looked surprised. 'Was I? I admit I get riled by the see-what-a-good-boy-am-I approach. It's unprofessional. There are two kinds of hard-working coppers, the ones who work for the job and the ones who work for promotion.'

The usually phlegmatic Kersey was moved to warmth. 'Don't I know it! I was the first sort and I had to wait until I'd turned forty to make inspector; Rowse has managed it before he's thirty. If I had my time to go over again, I know which I'd be!'

A wry grin. 'Perhaps you're right, but it won't hurt young Rowse to wonder for a bit what more he must do to inherit eternal life.'

The two men had worked together for several years and they understood each other's moods so that much could be said without words.

Kersey lit a cigarette. 'You're worried about this girl, sir, otherwise you wouldn't be here like this. The locals were coping very well. Now, if she turns up bright and smiling in the morning we shall have egg on our faces.'

Wycliffe snapped: 'You think I'd care about that?' Then, more calmly: 'I am worried, Doug. She's been missing for forty-eight hours with no news of any sort. I agree the local lads started well but we need a wider approach. If she's dead, then her body is hidden and may take weeks or months to find. We've got to try another line. Who might her hypothetical attacker have been? I know that sounds wide open, but it looks very much as though she disappeared on her way home, using a little-known field path —and that suggests a local, probably someone she knew.'

'So?'

'So we've got to get to know her, through her family, her school, her friends — and her enemies if she has any. The schools are on holiday but find out which teachers knew her best and try to locate them. And when you talk to the boy try to draw him out. It looks as though he's lied but that doesn't make him a liar. Anyway I can't see this as a boy–girl thing, but he may know something without realising it. Then there's gossip. Cook up some excuse for a house-to-house where it's most likely to be profitable.

'Anyway, who've you got in your team?'

'At the moment, Dixon, Curnow and Shaw. Lucy Lane is winding up the paperwork on her arson case and she could come down in the morning if she's needed. Shaw is fixing accommodation and Curnow has gone to bring in the boy.'

37

Wycliffe said: 'I think Shaw must look for suitable premises for an Incident Room; this tin box isn't going to do us for long.'

Shaw was the squad's collator and administrative officer.

'You think this is going to be a long haul?'

'It looks that way to me.'

A pause, then: 'Are you staying on the case, sir?'

'Me? No, I'm going back tonight. This is your case.'

Kersey grinned but said nothing.

Wycliffe was looking out of the little window, trying to get the feel of the place. On the quay a couple of fishermen squatted, mending their nets, like James and John, the sons of Zebedee, two thousand years ago, except that their nets were orange and green nylon and there was little chance of Jesus happening along.

DC Curnow arrived with Ralph Martin in tow. Curnow was obviously surprised to see his chief. 'The boy, Martin, sir.'

'I'm Chief Superintendent Wycliffe, this is Inspector Kersey. Sit down.'

The boy sat on the upholstered bench, on the other side of the table from the policemen; he sat with bowed head, hands resting on his thighs, near the end of his tether.

Kersey said: 'I've read your statement about what happened on Saturday but we now have evidence that you did not tell the truth. You said that you went after Hilda but that you did not find her.'

Martin gave no sign that he had heard.

'You were seen talking to her by the stile at the beginning of the Tregelles field path.'

The boy raised his head and stared with unfocused eyes out of the window, across the harbour. 'All right, I admit it. I'd already been a bit of the way along the coast path without seeing her so I thought I'd try the fields, though I didn't think she'd go that way.'

'Why not?'

He shook his head. 'I don't know; she would never walk that way with me. I thought it was because she didn't like passing her aunt's place; the families don't get on. Anyway, when I got there, she was sitting on the stile. I asked her what she was doing and she said she wanted a chance to think.'

The boy's arrival at the Incident Van in the charge of a policeman would have been observed all around the harbour; now eyes would be watching to see him leave, either free, or again with a policeman, perhaps in handcuffs.

'And after meeting her like that you still said you thought she'd gone home by bus.'

He made a gesture of helplessness. 'The passengers heard her say what she was going to do. If I said different it would mean I'd seen her.'

'You were afraid to admit seeing her because you knew what had happened.'

'No!' His temper flared but subsided at once. 'I just didn't want to talk about it.'

'You didn't want to talk about it! What did you talk about on the stile?'

'About the baby and what we should do.'

'Together?'

A long pause. 'That was what I wanted.'

'And Hilda?'

Wycliffe saw the boy's expression change from vague distress to dogged obstinacy.

'I'm not going to say any more.' He was near to tears.

'Did she say what she was going to do when you left her?'

'No, but I saw her set out along the field path so it seemed obvious.'

'Were you afraid that she might take her own life?'

'No! . . . She didn't, did she?'

'We don't know that she's dead. Why would anyone want to kill her?'

He brought his hands together, fingers tightly clenched. 'If I knew . . .'

'Yes?'

'Nothing.'

'You realize that you are bound to be a suspect, concerned in her disappearance? You lied to the police on two occasions; perhaps you are lying still. It's possible that you walked along the field path with her, that you quarrelled and that you — '

The boy turned to face Wycliffe, his fists clenched. In a harsh voice he said: 'You think that she's dead — that's what you're saying, isn't it?'

'We are saying that we have to look at every possibility, that you are, as far as we know now, the last person to have seen her, and that you are not helping yourself or us by lying or withholding information.'

Martin remained rigid and tense for a little longer then, suddenly, he relaxed, his whole body seemed to sag. 'Think what you like!' And, after a pause, he added: 'And do what you like.'

Kersey said: 'We're not playing games, lad. Don't get the wrong idea. We're trying to make it easy for you but there are other ways. We've got some more questions; you answer them here or you will be taken to the nearest police station and held until you give a satisfactory account of yourself.'

It was strange, this little drama being played out while the evening calm settled over the harbour and village. In the cafés and restaurants along the quay people were browsing over menus. The tide was at flood, but because it was the middle of the neaps, the moored craft rode well below the level of the quays. In some of them men were tinkering with engines or swabbing down the planking. Gulls spaced themselves on railings, on gunnels, and perched on mastheads, beady eyed, and still.

The boy made a gesture of resignation. 'All right, what do you want?'

Wycliffe put the question. 'Hilda is pregnant; is it your child?'

He flushed. 'Of course it's mine. What are you trying to say?'

'I'm asking the questions. How long have you been having sex with her?'

'Not long.' Sullen.

'How long — a month? A year?'

He was massaging his thighs with restless hands. Once or twice he seemed on the point of speaking, then changed his mind. Finally he said: 'It was the first time.'

'Was it the first time she had had sex with anyone?'

He did not answer at once, then he said: 'That's her business.'

'It was; now it's ours too. Answer the question.'

40

'I think she might have had sex before . . . But she wasn't — I mean she wasn't . . .'

Wycliffe exchanged glances with Kersey then he said: 'I'm going to leave you with Mr Curnow, the officer who brought you here. You will have the chance to make a fresh statement and I suggest that you tell the whole truth this time.'

'Shall I be allowed to go then?'

'Perhaps.'

Chapter Three

Monday evening (continued)

At Tregelles Farm Jane Rule was preparing a meal. Early evening sunlight filtered through the murky window-panes to form a shadowy grid pattern on the opposite wall. Two places were laid on the kitchen table and there was a tray, set with a bowl, a spoon and a slice of bread. A stew simmered on the stove in a saucepan covered with a plate. Little spurts of steam escaped from time to time causing the plate to chatter.

A bare, comfortless room: a slate floor covered in part by fibre matting; yellow painted walls and chocolate-brown woodwork. A black-and-white border collie and a tabby cat slept in amity on the hearth rug; the dog crouched, head on paws, the cat sprawled. An alarm clock on the mantelpiece clicked the moments away between two china dogs.

Jane Rule, gaunt and grey, stood, monumentally still, a ladle in one hand, like an automaton awaiting the signal to go through its routine.

A sound of boots grating on the scraper outside and her son came in: Clifford Rule was built like a heavyweight wrestler but his cheeks were smooth and rosy and he looked out on the world through eyes that were childlike in their innocence, uncritical, accepting whatever they saw. He wore a grey shirt tucked into cord trousers and he smelt of the farmyard.

Neither mother nor son spoke. Clifford went to the sink and washed with a great deal of spluttering. His mother, as though released from her immobility, began to ladle the stew into bowls, including a little for the bowl on the tray.

Clifford, drying himself, watched his mother with interest. 'How long you going to keep doing that?'

His mother snapped: 'Shut up, Clifford! Sit down and have your supper.'

Clifford sat and his mother placed a bowl of stew in front of him. 'You start while I take this up.'

She carried the tray to the stairs which made an angled ascent in one corner of the room. A moment or two later, floorboards creaked overhead and, after a brief interval, she came down again without the tray.

'I told you to start!' She took her place at the table and, in movements which seemed to be synchronized, they crumbled bread on the plastic table covering, picked up their spoons, and began their meal.

'Did you see the police?'

Clifford paused, and thought, his spoon half-way to his lips. 'That was yesterday.'

'They've been back.'

He put down his spoon and turned to his mother with anxious eyes. 'What did they come back for?'

'They wanted to look round.'

'But they looked everywhere yesterday: they had sticks and they poked in all the ditches and in the hedges, they — ' Clifford was becoming excited so that his words came tumbling over each other.

His mother spoke sharply: 'Slow down, boy! All they wanted was to look round the buildings.'

'The buildings.' He looked at his mother, open-mouthed. 'Did they come in the house?'

'Yes.'

He raised his eyes to the ceiling. 'Upstairs?'

'Yes.'

'The dairy?'

'Yes.'

The woman dripped information like a leaking tap. There were long pauses between the questions.

'They didn't — '

'No!'

'Did they ask questions?'

'No different to yesterday. Eat your food!'

For several minutes they ate in silence while the shadowy grid pattern crept slowly up the wall and the beam of sunlight was alive with gleaming particles of dust.

'She was here, too. The Innes woman, in her wheelchair.'

'What did she want?' He was anxious again.

'Quizzing about the police. You don't have to worry about her. I can deal with her sort.'

Clifford frowned. 'Mr Innes is good to me.'

'Good to you! Good to you because he gives you half what you're worth when you work for him. I tell you, boy, you'd do better to keep away from that lot!'

When Ralph Martin had been taken into another cubicle, Wycliffe studied the Ordnance map pinned to the wall; he could never begin to come to terms with a case until he had been over the terrain; until, like any naturalist, he had done his fieldwork. To bring in a witness or a suspect for questioning was like caging an animal in order to study it. Something might be learned of behaviour under stress but it is no way to arrive at any understanding of motives, of responses, and of the way the individual fits into the pattern of other lives.

He turned to Kersey. 'These people at the farm — Tregelles — I'm going to take a look at them. I'll drive home later this evening and I'll be in touch in the morning.'

He walked along the quay and through the square, where most of the real shops were, then he followed one of the narrow streets leading away from the harbour. A resurrected villager of a century ago would have had no difficulty in recognising his village, nor in identifying most of the buildings. The transition from fish to tourists (mercifully not complete) had so far been accomplished without wholesale devastation.

He was leaving the village behind as the road began to climb, fields on his left, trees on his right, then the entrance to the caravan park, and an arched sign: 'Tregwythen Leisure and

Tourist Park'. Through the arch there was a prospect of terraced slopes with trees and shrubs doing their best to hide the caravans.

He entered the site, passed the shop and reception building on his left, and a drive leading to a dwelling house on his right. A metalled road wound pleasantly, following the valley, with tiered stands for the vans on either side. The sun was still well above the trees but the light was already turning golden, promising one of those summer evenings of infinite calm.

The caravanners were at home, children played on the grass, fathers too; muted radios competed without aggression and, through open doorways, Wycliffe glimpsed women preparing meals on bottled-gas stoves.

The road ended in a footpath where the trees began and there was a perceptible chill as he entered the wood. Sunlight slanted through the branches creating an atmosphere of solemnity and the silence was complete. The path divided into two: a left-hand fork which followed the course of a small stream, and a right-hand one which climbed a gentle slope where trees were sparser and there were outcrops of moss-covered rocks. Wycliffe chose the path by the stream.

Almost at once the path widened into a track and then into a clearing with the stream on one side and a disused quarry on the other. The quarry, gouged and blasted out of the hillside, was now flooded, creating an extensive pool at the foot of cliff-like walls. At the top, thirty or forty feet up, gorse bushes in their second flowering formed a ring of acid yellow against the blue sky and, although the slope was steep, more bushes and even sapling trees had found a root-hold in and on its crevices and ledges.

The surface of the pool was patchily covered with bright green weed; the gaps, where dark water showed, were almost certainly due to the flounderings of the police frogman earlier in the day.

It was a strangely still and sombre place until, suddenly, a flock of chattering starlings flew in to settle on the ledges, then with equal abruptness, as though at a signal, they took off again in a flurry of wings.

Wycliffe continued along the track which rose steadily, leaving the course of the stream and the quarry behind. The trees closed in again but, as he reached the top of the rise, they gave way to low hedges and the track became a lane. He had a view over the whole countryside. Young bullocks and sheep grazed the adjacent fields. To his left, in the middle distance, a wedge of sea cut into the profile of the land, while in all other directions there were rolling fields, the occasional house or farm and, at one point, a church tower.

A farm gate labelled 'Tregelles' and a stile both led directly into a farmyard. A finger-post on the stile pointed 'Footpath to Gorran Haven', so that anyone using the path had to pass through the farmyard. But the lane continued on past the farm and he could see at least two more houses along it before it joined the Gorran road a quarter of a mile away.

If Hilda Clemo had set out along this path from the Haven, how far had she got? Had she reached the farm? The quarry? Or had she, for some reason, followed the lane to its junction with the road?

The farmyard was cluttered with rubbish and straw; a museum-piece tractor and a veteran Morris Minor stood in an open shed. Hens pecked among the cobbles and there were hutches against a sheltered wall where rabbits shuffled and squeaked. A shaggy, black-and-white collie came out of the house, barking and growling by turns, and was followed by a heavily built man, dark, with a ruddy complexion like a burnished apple.

'You want something, mister?'

His manner was in no way aggressive; he spoke softly as though his only wish was to make himself agreeable.

'Isn't this a public footpath to Gorran Haven?'

'People don't come this way much; they mostly go round by the coast path.'

'But Hilda Clemo came this way on Saturday afternoon.'

The dark eyes became fearful. 'If you come from the newspapers I don't know anything, mister.'

'I'm not from the newspapers. I'm Detective Chief Superintendent Wycliffe.' He showed his warrant card. 'Are you Mr Rule?'

The man hesitated. 'Yes, that's me.' He was clearly worried, unsure what to say or do. 'The police was here this morning and they was here yesterday.' His mind wrestled with the problem of saying, politely, that there was no point in this further visit. 'They searched everywhere but they didn't find anything . . . I think Hilda must've gone another way.' He nodded in approval, pleased with this idea. 'I think that's what she done.' His manner was almost pleading.

'What other way?'

This was too much for him; he looked back into the house as though in the hope of support but none came and, resigned, he said: 'You best come in and talk to mother.'

Wycliffe followed him into the kitchen. Cold comfort farm. A thin, grey-haired woman was washing dishes at an earthenware sink.

'It's another policeman . . .'

The woman had taken no apparent notice so far; now she turned, wiped her hands on a limp, grubby towel and said: 'This is the third time we've had the police. But we've told all we know, and that's nothing.'

Her voice was harsh and she spoke slowly as one unaccustomed to much conversation.

Her son stood just inside the door. He had taken from his pocket a clasp knife with several blades and he repeatedly opened one of the blades to let it spring back with a loud click.

'If your niece came by the field path on Saturday afternoon she must have come through your yard.'

'Perhaps, but that don't signify. We didn't see her.'

'At about five that afternoon, where were you both?'

Jane Rule stood, immobile, her face expressionless, not a muscle moved; he had rarely seen anyone capable of such statuesque inertia. Even when she spoke, movement seemed confined to her lips. 'Clifford was out in the fields somewhere — '

'I was over to Bassett's — that's a field — mending the gate . . . To keep the sheep in.'

'Near the path?'

'No, the path don't come near Bassett's.'

47

His mother said: 'And I was lying down upstairs before cooking supper. I'm on my feet from six in the morning.'

'But the dog would have barked, surely?'

'The dog was with Clifford.'

'The dog was with me — to keep the sheep in like while I was mending the gate.'

The silence and the stillness which seemed to pervade the whole landscape closed in again, punctuated by the clicks from Clifford's knife, and if it had been left to the Rules it might have continued indefinitely.

'Does your niece pass this way often?'

'If she does, I don't see her. Perhaps now and then.'

'Does she ever call in when she's passing?'

'We're not on terms; we just pass the time of day.'

Clifford said, with obvious regret: 'Hilda used to come here but not now.'

His mother snapped: 'That was a long time ago.'

'What about your sister-in-law? Where was she on Saturday afternoon?'

'Up in her room.'

Clifford tried to join in once more: 'She don't come down much except when she's for going out.'

Jane Rule ignored him: 'Agnes — my sister-in-law — is seventy-seven and she's gone queer in the head; senile, they call it.'

'She thinks she's still a girl,' Clifford said.

'She sits by her window for hours, watching the sea, just watching, waiting for Ernie Pascoe's boat to come in. Ernie was her intended and he was drowned out fishing nearly sixty years ago.'

Jane Rule's grey eyes held his gaze and he was aware of a strange disquiet. A woman ground down by circumstance; she had good features and, at one time, she must have been an attractive woman; now her habitual expression was one of sullen melancholy. Only occasionally the eyes came alive in a momentary flash of resentment. Wycliffe felt sorry for her.

'That's very sad.'

The woman seemed to react to his sympathy. 'The trouble is, although she spends so much time in her room, you can't rely on it. Sometimes she'll creep downstairs and wander off, and we have to go looking for her.'

'So she's all right on her legs?'

'There's nothing wrong with her legs — it's her head.'

The subject seemed to be exhausted and Wycliffe tried another tack. 'This lane which leads out to the road — I see there are other houses along it.'

'A couple.'

'Who lives in them?'

Jane Rule pouted. 'In the first one there's a man and a woman called Innes — that's if they're married. She paints pictures and he's supposed to be some sort of writer.'

'Are they good neighbours?'

A barely perceptible lift of the shoulders but no reply.

'The other house, nearly out to the road, is the Moyles' place. There's a whole tribe of Moyles and the eldest boy works down at the caravan site.' The first time she had volunteered information unasked.

It was depressing: the woman, bleak and sombre, with her feeble-minded son making his pathetic effort at sociability. The woman was resentful and sullen, but wasn't her defensive attitude more than explained by her hard life? A widow with a half-wit son and a demented old woman, struggling to keep the farm going and make ends meet. Of course it was possible that Clifford Rule had raped and murdered the missing girl and that his mother had done, and was doing, all she could to conceal the crime.

'. . . a bit soft in the head but amiable, never caused any trouble' — The local verdict, but Wycliffe, who read psychology more from a sense of duty than conviction, knew that statistically the mentally subnormal male shows a greater proneness to sex crimes than to other forms of criminality.

'Is this farm yours, Mrs Rule?'

'I'm the tenant.'

'And your landlord?'

'I don't see it's your business but I suppose you can find out easy enough; the farm belongs to the Clemos.'

Wycliffe had run out of questions and, still uneasy, took himself off. Clifford and the dog escorted him to the yard but the woman returned to her dishes.

He did not cross the yard to the other stile but decided to follow the lane which would take him past the neighbouring houses to the road.

The first of the Rules' neighbours lived about four hundred yards along the lane in a substantial, large, fairly modern bungalow, surrounded by a field of mown grass. In a corner of the field a clump of ageing pines looked as though they had been lifted from a Japanese print. A grey *deux chevaux* was parked in front of the house.

Wycliffe went to the front door which stood open to a tiled passage. As there was neither bell nor knocker he rapped with his knuckles. No one answered so he knocked louder and a girlish voice called: 'There's someone at the door, Tristan! Will you go, please?'

A brief interval, and a man appeared at the end of the passage: tall, slim, dark, and thirtyish. 'Good evening . . .' Tentative.

'Chief Superintendent Wycliffe . . . Mr Innes?'

'Yes, indeed. I'm glad you've come, Chief Superintendent. I intended to contact someone. Do come in.'

His manner was amiable, flattering in its diffidence; he walked with a slight scholarly stoop and his movements, probably because of his height, were rather slow and self-conscious.

'In here.'

The room which ran the whole depth of the house seemed to be a combination of sitting-room and library. The floor-to-ceiling bookcases, with their moulded cornices, disguised the fact that it was part of a modern bungalow. With a few 'good' pieces of furniture they created an impression of elegance. The over-large window was discreetly cut down to size by brocaded curtains, and the decor was subdued. Indian miniatures hung where there was an exposed wall and the carpet on the floor was Persian, Tree-of-Life design.

Either Innes's writing and lecturing must be very profitable or there were other resources.

'Do sit down . . . This, of course, is about Hilda. Is there any news?' The brown eyes were solemn, concerned.

Wycliffe was momentarily put off his stroke. 'No. Do I understand that you know Hilda?'

A brief smile. 'Yes, indeed. In the past six or seven months we've seen quite a lot of her.'

'How did that come about?'

A slight movement of the long, pale hands. 'As part of my work I travel about the south west, lecturing on aspects of the history of art and it happened that I was invited to Hilda's school. She was sufficiently interested to come here a few days later. It became obvious that she had a quite exceptional intelligence and my wife and I were glad to encourage her.'

Innes's speech was meticulous and unhurried, every syllable received its full value, each phrase and each sentence was followed by a distinct pause so that one could almost see the marks of punctuation. Everything about the man conveyed an impression of deliberation yet Wycliffe sensed that, underneath, there was tension.

'She comes here often?'

A pursing of the lips: 'Once a week? Sometimes more often.'

'Do you give her lessons?'

'Oh dear me, no! Nothing like that. We talk, we listen to music, we read poetry together and we look at and discuss pictures.'

'The three of you?'

A shrewd look. 'Yes, the three of us; my wife is very fond of Hilda. Hilda wants to broaden her horizons and we may be able to help her to do that by offering her understanding companionship and conversation.'

'You said that you were intending to make contact with us.'

'I was. I wanted to tell you just what I've told you now. It happens that I was away yesterday when the police called — in fact, I left home on Saturday evening and only returned this afternoon. I gather that my wife may not have realized how seriously the police regarded Hilda's disappearance — '

51

'So you were at home on Saturday afternoon?'

'Oh, yes. I was due to lecture at a weekend school in Exeter on Sunday, and this morning I had an appointment at the university. I spent Saturday and Sunday nights with a friend at Tedburn St Mary near Exeter.'

'But you didn't see Hilda at all on Saturday?'

'Yes, I did on Saturday afternoon — '

'Here?'

'No, I was taking the dog for a run across the fields in the direction of Gorran Haven and I met Hilda coming this way. I asked her if she was calling in at our place and she said that she was not; she was on her way home.'

'Your wife didn't mention this to the officer yesterday.'

'She didn't know. I don't suppose it occurred to me to say that I'd met Hilda, there was nothing unusual about the encounter.'

'When did you first hear of her disappearance?'

'Only when I returned home this afternoon.'

'What time did you see her on Saturday?'

He frowned. 'I can't say exactly but it must have been shortly before five.'

'Did she seem her usual self?'

Hesitation. 'I think so. Perhaps a little subdued but Hilda is a moody girl.'

The room faced north and already the light indoors was growing dim; the silence was absolute. Innes sat, his long legs crossed, waiting politely for further questions. Wycliffe was in no hurry; by allowing a silence to become uncomfortable one could provoke questions which were often more informative than answers.

It was only when Wycliffe was beginning to think that he had lost the silent battle that the question came: 'Do you really think that Hilda has come to some harm?'

Wycliffe did not answer directly. 'You must know her at least as well as most people; is it likely that she would walk out on her family, taking nothing with her, and telling no one?'

Innes shook his head. 'No, I must say that it isn't.' After a pause he asked: 'Are you suggesting that something happened to her between here and her home on Saturday afternoon?'

52

'It's hardly a suggestion. If you saw her near here at five o'clock and she didn't arrive home, it seems a logical inference.'

'Yes, of course. It's just that I find it hard to imagine what could have happened.'

'Do you know that she is pregnant?' Wycliffe put the question with apparent casualness.

'*Pregnant*?'

'Confirmed by her doctor on Saturday morning.'

'Oh, dear! I had no idea. Poor girl! Do you think her pregnancy could have anything to do with her disappearance?'

'Do you?'

Innes looked put out. 'I know nothing of the circumstances but I hardly think Hilda would do anything foolish or dramatic if that is what you mean.'

It seemed that they might be entering upon another lull when there was a sound of rubber wheels in the passage. Innes got to his feet and hurried to open the door to a woman in a wheelchair. She wore a grey smock, heavily spattered with paint. She was so small that at first sight Wycliffe took her for a child.

'I hope I'm not intruding?'

'No, Polly, of course not! Come in and meet Chief Superintendent Wycliffe. He's come about Hilda.' He turned to Wycliffe. 'My wife — as you will see for yourself, she paints.'

Very skilfully she manoeuvred her chair to a convenient position. The chair must have been made specially; it was both narrower and higher than is usual, presumably to give greater mobility and compensate for her own lack of height.

She was looking at Wycliffe with anxious eyes. 'A chief superintendent?'

Innes said: 'Yes, the police are taking Hilda's disappearance very seriously indeed, Polly.' He turned to Wycliffe. 'My wife and I misjudged the situation, we thought that this was no more than a teenage escapade, a consequence, perhaps, of a family row. Young people react so dramatically these days . . .' Then to his wife: 'The fact is, Mr Wycliffe has just told me that Hilda is pregnant.'

'Pregnant! Poor girl!'

Polly Innes was like a perfectly proportioned scale-model of a woman. She must have been less than five feet tall and very slender. Her skin was pale, its paleness accentuated by straight black hair which she wore at shoulder length. Her features had the perfection of a doll's but when her face was caught in the light from the window Wycliffe saw that she looked ill, her eyes were dark ringed and her face was drawn, almost haggard.

Wycliffe said: 'We don't think that Hilda left home of her own accord.'

There was a sharp intake of breath from Polly Innes but she said nothing; she looked from Wycliffe to her husband and back again.

Innes was reflective. 'I was very surprised to hear that Hilda is pregnant. My first reaction was that she is far too intelligent but, of course, that is foolish. Obviously there are times when intelligence is not enough.'

He looked at Wycliffe, perhaps to judge the effect of his remark, but Wycliffe was staring, dreamy eyed, at an Indian miniature which depicted an erotic encounter in a grove of blossoming trees. He was thinking that Polly Innes could have been the model for the woman in the painting.

His interest was not lost on Innes. 'The resemblance is striking, is it not?'

In a strained voice Polly Innes asked: 'Do you know the boy responsible for Hilda's pregnancy?'

Wycliffe shook his head. 'Not with certainty.' He changed the subject: 'In your conversations with her, what were your impressions? Do you see her as a highly intelligent but otherwise average schoolgirl? Or did any particular aspect of her character strike you so that you might tend to think of her as "the girl who . . ."?'

Innes smiled. '"The girl who . . ." I know exactly what you mean; and you have a point. But although we have spent many hours with Hilda I don't feel that I know her any better than I did after her first visit. At that time she allowed us to see something of herself, but what wasn't revealed then has been carefully guarded ever since.'

Polly Innes nodded agreement.

Innes went on: 'It was as though she had paid her subscription; a sort of psychological entrance fee, and that was that. I'm no psychologist but Hilda seems to put out feelers anticipating, almost inviting, a hostile response, and when the response is not hostile she becomes suspicious.' He looked at his wife. 'Isn't that so, Polly?'

'Oh, yes, quite so.' Words seem to come with difficulty as from one who is not following the conversation, preoccupied, perhaps by pain.

They talked for a little while longer, or Innes talked, and he agreed to come to the Incident Van to make a formal statement. He saw Wycliffe off at the gate.

The orange sun was low behind the pines creating a dramatic silhouette. At the last moment, as though the admission was somehow being forced from him, Innes said: 'My wife injured her spine in a car accident and she has bad days when she suffers a great deal. This is one of them.'

'I'm very sorry. You are able to leave her in the house alone when you go away?'

'Oh, yes. She feels well enough most of the time and she can get about with crutches, but it is an arduous and somewhat ungainly business so that she is unwilling to meet strangers except in her chair.'

A couple of hundred yards up the lane Wycliffe came to a ramshackle building where the lane joined the road. It was surrounded by an area of rough grass littered with the wrecks of cars and vans. In an open shed a young man, presumably a Moyle, was at work on another vehicle which looked in rather better shape.

Wycliffe was thinking about the Inneses; they left him with a sense of unreality, as though he had been watching a stage performance. The setting, their attitudes, their conversation, reminded him of actors following stage directions and a script. But there are plenty of people who more or less consciously cast themselves in certain roles and surround themselves with the appropriate props, often as a defence against something.

At least he had established that someone had seen the girl after Ralph Martin left her at the stile.

James Clemo lay on his bed, fully dressed, staring at the ceiling. Early evening sunshine flooded the room. A whisky bottle and glass stood, with the alarm clock, on his bedside table. The clock showed ten minutes past six.

The door opened and Esther came in but he gave no sign. She stood looking at him and the lines of her thin, pale face softened.

'Aren't you coming down?'

'No.'

'Alice has just come from the village; she says the police are questioning Ralph Martin again; they've got him in their van on the quay.'

He did not turn towards her but continued to stare at the ceiling. 'They're wasting their time; the boy didn't do it.'

'There's nothing to say that anybody "did it". We don't know that anything has happened to Hilda.'

Clemo made a weary gesture. 'You and I know well enough, Esther.'

Abruptly, he turned away from her and his body was shaken by sobs. For a moment it seemed that she was about to say something but she merely stood over him, her face full of concern, then she picked up the whisky bottle and left the room.

Chapter Four

Wycliffe arrived home in darkness and Helen came out into the drive while he was putting the car away. Their house, a former coastguard station, stood at least two good stone-throws from their nearest neighbour, overlooking the narrows where the river met the sea. Navigation lights twinkled in the channel and, upstream, the sky above the city blazed with a fierce orange glow.

Indoors, Helen said: 'Drink?'

'A small whisky.'

'Worried?' It was unusual for him to drink spirits.

'I suppose I am.'

In the remnant of their day they ate chicken sandwiches while watching a television serial about a poor rich family who, because the husband had thrown up his job, faced hard times, and were forced to sell their yacht. Their teenaged daughter took it badly, but her practically minded, caring brother got a job as a petrol-pump attendant. Granny would have helped but she had invested all her money in half a race horse which had gone lame.

As the credits rolled Wycliffe said: 'I suppose we should be thankful we don't have their problems.'

Helen switched off. 'Don't knock it. The dresses were pretty, so was the music, and you didn't have to think. What more do you want? Anyway, it's early to bed for you. Do you want anything?'

'What about cocoa?'

'You'll only say cocoa isn't what it was.'

'It isn't, but let's try it once more.'

He went to sleep while his mind played tricks, juggling with random fragments of his day. Later in the night he dreamed that he had been awakened by someone calling. In his dream he got out of bed and went to the window. Below him, standing on the grass, he saw Jane and Clifford Rule looking up at him. Although it was dark he could see every detail of their figures and faces. Clifford's features were blank and receptive but Jane was smiling and, for some reason, this angered him. In his dream he banged on the glass and shouted, but his efforts made no sound and the Rules did not move, nor did their expressions change. In his frustration Wycliffe awoke, confused and distressed.

The bedside clock showed two-fifteen. He listened, surprised to hear rain — the first for almost three weeks.

He lay awake, brooding, troubled by his visit to the farm and by his absurd dream. The truth was beginning to dawn on him: that he had been taken in. Jane Rule had been too clever for him — all her talk about her sister-in-law was surely out of character, it had come in response to his sympathy and served to divert his attention from something else. Or so it seemed to him now.

The Rules, mother and son, were recipe suspects, but of what did he suspect them? Were they responsible for Hilda Clemo's disappearance? Perhaps, but it was equally possible that they were attempting a cover-up of something quite different. Women like Jane Rule, shrewd about many things, were often vague about the role of the police, so that in the light of a dodgy tax return or a false claim for an agricultural subsidy any attention from them might seem threatening.

All the same . . .

He decided that he was unlikely to settle down to sleep in a hurry but the next thing he knew it was full daylight, seven o'clock, and Helen was getting up.

'You've been restless.'

'Sorry!'

'It's not your fault. Stay there and I'll bring you your coffee.'

At eight, when the Incident Van would be manned, he telephoned. 'Anything to report?'

'Nothing, sir.'

'Then give me the number of the place where Mr Kersey is staying.'

A minute or two later he was talking to Kersey. 'In the middle of the eggs and bacon?'

'I should be so lucky! I promised Joan to keep to toast and marmalade.'

'I'm coming down; I'll meet you at the van as soon as I can get there. What's the weather like?'

'Drizzle.'

'It's the same here.'

Wycliffe made a second call, this time to his deputy, John Scales, at home.

'Sorry to interrupt your breakfast, John. I want a discreet check on a chap called Tristan Innes . . . Yes, sounds like some character from a novelette, but he's real enough. He's a lecturer and writer on something or other, I'm not quite sure what, but he says he was lecturing at a weekend school in Exeter on Sunday and that he had an appointment at the university on Monday morning. Anything you can find out . . . He's probably a respectable academic so don't stir things . . .'

It was Kersey's first visit to the farm. Misty rain settled out of a leaden sky, the countryside was blotted out, and the prospect dismal. Hens scrabbled in the yard and one came stalking out through the open door of the house as they arrived. Kersey called: 'Anybody home?'

Jane Rule's harsh voice came from somewhere at the back. 'Who is it? What do you want?'

'Police.'

She came, glowering. 'Aren't we ever going to be left in peace?' Then she saw Wycliffe and her manner softened. 'Oh, it's you.'

'Is it all right if we come in?'

She withdrew from the doorway. 'If I said no, what difference would it make?'

'Your son is not at home, Mrs Rule?'

'What do you expect? He's got work to do.'

Wycliffe said: 'We want to check all the houses in the neighbourhood to make absolutely sure that the missing girl isn't being hidden — it's routine and we shan't hinder you . . .'

The room had a yeasty smell of warm dough and a pan stood in front of the solid-fuel range, covered by a cloth. On the table there were little heaps of vegetables and a bowl containing rabbit steaks, presumably soaking in salted water.

Jane Rule busied herself, riddling ash from the fire. She turned her head. 'You've got no right to search my house.'

Kersey said: 'You object? Something to hide?'

'I said, you've got no right.'

'It would be simple to get a warrant, but just a quick look round — it won't take more than two or three minutes.'

Kersey was half-way up the creaking stairs as he spoke. The woman dropped her poker and was about to protest but changed her mind. 'The old lady's in the room over this; she's asleep. I don't want her woke up yet; the only peace I get is when she's asleep.'

There were three bedrooms. The first was the son's, a small room overlooking the backyard: a single bed with grey blankets, a battered wardrobe, a chest of drawers, and a pervasive sour smell of unwashed clothing. On the top of the chest there was a veritable menagerie of little animals, carved from wood; and wood chips littered the floor. Wycliffe thought the carvings had vigour.

The second room was larger, a double bed, the furniture in better shape. There was proper bedding, and pictures on the walls — one, a framed photograph of a young couple; the girl was undoubtedly Jane, her features not yet hardened and her body still with its youthful curves. Kersey did a rapid and silent rummage.

In the third bedroom, the old lady's, the furniture was almost elegant, walnut, with maple inlay, and there were pictures on the walls here too — paintings in gilded, swept frames. The double bed was covered with a patchwork quilt of quality and the pillow, placed in the middle, was approximately white.

A small grey head rested on the pillow, the face hidden by the sheet. The old woman's body made a scarcely discernible mound under the clothes. On a bedside table there was a tray with a used cup and saucer and a plate with a few crumbs.

Kersey repeated his search tactics and Wycliffe began to feel foolish. What were they looking for? Hilda Clemo's body in the wardrobe?

They turned to leave, and were confronted by Jane Rule in the doorway. She spoke in a low voice: 'I hope you're satisfied!'

If she had not chanced to bar their way they would have left the room without another glance. As it was, Wycliffe turned and looked back. He was struck by something odd about the figure in the bed. He walked over, and heard Jane Rule catch her breath as he did so. Gently, he lifted the bedclothes and uncovered the head of a dummy, fitted with a grey wig, and a rolled blanket, roughly mounded to represent a human figure.

He turned to the woman, utterly at a loss. He said: 'Your sister-in-law?' He had not intended irony but he could think of nothing else to say.

'I've never hurt anybody in my life. You can say what you like!'

Wycliffe leaned forward in his chair, his arms resting on the kitchen table. 'All right, you've never hurt anybody, so where is your sister-in-law?'

Jane Rule sat, bolt upright, opposite her questioner. She looked him straight in the eyes, betraying not the slightest sign of any nervousness. The little piles of vegetables and the bowl of rabbit steaks were still on the table and the pan of dough still stood in front of the range.

Jane Rule said: 'She wandered off. I told you yesterday the trouble I was having with Agnes.'

'When did she go? This morning, before we arrived?'

She stopped herself from giving a too-ready answer and took time to consider. 'No, she was gone when you was here yesterday.'

'When did she go?'

For once her gaze faltered and she looked vaguely around the poorly lit room. 'Where's he gone? The other one?'

'Mr Kersey is searching your outbuildings.'

'They've done that before — looking for the girl.'

The drizzle had turned to real rain; they could hear it drumming on the corrugated-iron roofs in the yard, and water streamed down the window from a damaged gutter. The stove gave off a humid, drowsy warmth, and the light in the kitchen was dim, steely-grey, obliterating what little colour there might have been.

Wycliffe asked: 'Could we have a light on?'

Without a word she got up and flicked a switch near the door. A naked bulb cast a yellowish glow over the table and failed to reach beyond it.

'I asked you when your sister-in-law "wandered off".'

'Friday — Friday morning it was.'

'And you didn't report her missing?'

'Clifford and me searched for her. She usually made for Drum Point where she used to do her courting when she was a girl — '

'You didn't find her. Why didn't you report it so that a proper search could be made?'

She was less sure of herself now. Her clasped hands made small uneasy movements. 'I thought she would come back and I didn't want the Clemos saying I hadn't looked after her — because I had.'

'She went on Friday morning and it's now Tuesday — that's four days. Are you still expecting her back?'

She looked at him but said nothing.

Wycliffe tried again. 'Your sister-in-law, Agnes, was a sister to Mrs Elinor Clemo who was buried on Friday, is that right?'

'Yes.'

'Isn't it an odd coincidence that she should disappear on the day of her sister's funeral?'

'I think Agnes was upset about Elinor; it was hard to tell whether she understood — whether she took it in that her sister was dead, but she was unsettled.'

'Why did you try to make it look as though she was still in the bed upstairs?'

'In case somebody came.'

Wycliffe was puzzled by the woman; she was by no means stupid but she seemed to reason from her own singular premises. He sat back in his chair. 'I'm sorry, Mrs Rule, but I don't believe much of what you've told me. You would be sensible to — '

They were interrupted by a knock at the door which opened, and Kersey came to stand just inside, out of the rain. The brim of his fisherman's hat dripped on his shoulders and his waterproof dripped on the slate floor. 'Sorry to interrupt; I'm through outside except for a lean-to building at the back which is padlocked.'

Wycliffe turned to the woman: 'Will you let Mr Kersey have the key?'

'He's talking about the old dairy; you don't need a key, you can go through from the scullery. You won't find whatever you're looking for, but you can look; it's all the same to me.'

If anything she seemed relieved by the interruption.

'This way . . .'

They followed her into a damp, cavernous scullery where there was a tap, a trough sink, a fuel bin, an antique wash boiler, and a chest freezer. She opened another plank door and they found themselves in a narrow passage between stacks of furniture, a number of crates, and rolls of carpet; it was like a removals warehouse. The furniture was stored, one piece on another, with layers of felt between. There was little light because the windows were blocked by the furniture and by the crates.

'This all belongs to Agnes. She kept house for her brother. When he died the house was let and she moved in with me and brought the furniture with her. You've seen some of it up in her room.'

'What's in the crates?'

'How should I know? Pictures, china, ornaments, that sort of thing, I suppose. They had a big house. Henry made money — and spent it, gambled away most of it.'

'What happens to all this if your sister-in-law is dead?'

'I suppose that depends on her will — if she made one.'

Wycliffe felt frustrated. But what had he expected? He had set out in search of a missing girl and been side-tracked by this infuriating woman. And yet . . .

Kersey turned to him and shrugged. They filed back into the scullery. It happened that as Wycliffe reached the door the freezer motor cut in, drawing his attention to the battered, rusty chest which must have been among the earliest made. The lid had been fitted, unskilfully, with a brass padlock which looked new.

'What do you keep in there?'

Jane Rule looked at him. 'What would you think? The same as your wife keeps in hers, I suppose.'

'Get the key, please.'

She stood her ground. 'How much more do I have to put up with? You come in here and take over my house — '

'Get the key or we shall break it open.'

She reached behind the freezer and came up with a small steel key which she handed to Wycliffe.

Wycliffe felt strangely reluctant, but he inserted the key in the lock; it turned easily, he removed the padlock, flipped back the hasp, and lifted the lid.

It was like looking down at a crouched burial on some archaeological site. A small, anonymous figure rested on its side, almost filling the chest, knees drawn up almost to the chin. The whole body except the head and hands was swathed in some garment, perhaps a nightdress, now rigid with frost. The flesh, where any could be seen, was grey and appeared to have shrivelled so that the bones were unduly prominent; and the sparse grey hair protruded from the scalp in frozen wisps.

Wycliffe lowered the lid. Jane Rule was standing in the doorway to the kitchen, her back towards them.

'Here's Clifford: I don't want him mixed up in this.'

They heard the front door open and shut, and as they moved into the kitchen Clifford was there, taking off an old trench-coat that was almost waterlogged.

He looked from one to the other with apprehension. 'What's going on?'

His mother said: 'You keep your mouth shut! I'll do the talking.'

Wycliffe trotted out the obligatory warning: 'I have to tell you,

Mrs Rule, and you, Mr Rule, that you do not have to say anything but what you do say may be taken down and used in evidence.'

The four of them were seated round the kitchen table; the clock on the mantelpiece showed five minutes past eleven. The dog and cat were asleep in front of the stove. Jane Rule was once more in complete possession of herself; she sat quite still, her grey eyes on Wycliffe but showing no particular concern.

Clifford, his great body hunched, arms on the table, played with his clasp knife. With total concentration he lifted a blade between finger and thumb, released it, and let it snap back into place. The clicks came with the regularity of a metronome.

Jane Rule said: 'I've said before, I've never hurt anybody, and it's true.'

'Then what happened to your sister-in-law?'

'She died.'

'Of what did she die?'

'She was seventy-seven: people don't live for ever.'

'When did she die?'

A momentary hesitation, then: 'Friday — Friday morning.'

'The day of her sister's funeral.'

The woman said nothing.

'As I've told you, you don't have to answer my questions at this stage. In fact, you might be well advised to get in touch with a solicitor.'

'I don't need a solicitor.'

'Very well. What happened? How did Agnes Rule die?'

She gave the first sign of renewed disquiet, stroking the plastic table covering with the palm of her hand.

'She was sitting in that chair by the stove.' She pointed to a wooden armchair with a slatted back. 'One minute she was all right, then she started coughing, like if something had gone the wrong way — she was always sucking sweets. Then, before I could get to her, she just tumbled out of the chair onto the mat and she was gone. Heart, I suppose it was.'

'You didn't call a doctor?'

'He couldn't have done anything — she was dead.'

Once more Clifford's knife snapped back into place. Without raising his eyes he said: 'She was dead; anybody could see she was dead.'

His mother rounded on him. 'Shut up, Clifford! And put that damned knife away, you're getting on my nerves!'

Like a scolded child Clifford slipped the knife into his pocket and sat, staring at the table.

'Didn't you know, Mrs Rule, that you were under a legal obligation to obtain a certificate stating the cause of death, and to register the death?'

She remained silent.

'Why didn't you?'

She was looking down at the table, not meeting his eyes, then she asked, with unusual diffidence: 'Will they be able to tell?'

'Tell what?'

'What she died of.'

'That depends on the condition of the body and the actual cause of death.'

'What will happen to me?' Her eyes were on her son, for once she was vulnerable; her manner, bleak.

Wycliffe was gentle: 'I shall arrange for you and your son to be taken to St Austell police station where you will be asked further questions and invited to make statements. If you wish, a solicitor may be present during the questioning.'

'What then? Will they let us come home again?'

Wycliffe hesitated then he said: 'It is unlikely that you will be kept overnight. Just one more question: surely your sister-in-law had friends? Did no one visit her?'

Jane was running her fingers over the plastic table covering. 'You don't have friends when you're old. Anyway, nobody's been to see her for a long time — six months, at least.'

'And before that?'

'There was the old lady,' Clifford said. 'She used to come Sundays.'

Jane Rule sighed. 'He's talking about Lily Armitage. She used to come every Sunday but she got arthritis so bad she couldn't get about any more.'

'Where does she live?'

'In the village, if she's still there — Albert Place, but I couldn't tell you the number.'

Tuesday morning (continued)

Their police car was parked in the lane, by the entrance to the farmyard which had become a sea of mud.

Wycliffe said: 'Drop me off at the caravan site — at the house. You get back and arrange about the Rules. There's no great rush; they won't run away. Send Curnow with them.'

They had to make a broad circuit to reach the entrance to the caravan site. The rain fell vertically, bouncing off the car, and the roads were deserted. Kersey drove up to the front door and waited until someone answered Wycliffe's ring.

'Yes?'

The woman was painfully thin; her hair, drawn back in a wispy pony-tail, left her face looking strangely naked. She wore a shapeless grey frock which draped rather than clothed her figure.

Wycliffe introduced himself. 'You are . . .?'

'I'm Esther Clemo. You've found Hilda?' Peremptory.

'I'm sorry — no.'

Her features which had been momentarily animated relapsed into a sullen mould. 'They're all out. What do you want?'

'To talk to you.'

She hesitated, then: 'You'd better come in.' Her voice was harsh and her manner abrasive.

He was taken into the drawing-room — a relic of times past: framed family photographs and colour prints of Highland stags on faded flock wallpaper; an open fireplace stuffed with crinkly red paper, and a huge Canton jar of dried grasses in the fender.

Esther stood, her hands clasped against her abdomen, and waited.

'Don't you think we might sit down?'

She shrugged and pointed to a chair, then sat herself on the edge of another.

'I've just come from Tregelles.'

'What about it?'

'This morning we found Agnes Rule's body.'

'Her *body*?'

'Yes, she's been dead for some time — several days at least.'

Esther was obviously shocked. Once or twice she was on the point of saying something but changed her mind, then: 'I suppose she wandered off and they didn't find her until too late?' She seemed anxious that this should be the explanation and fearful that it would not.

'It wasn't like that, Miss Clemo. We found Agnes's body in the Rules' freezer.'

A quick glance but otherwise no response; the woman seemed afraid of giving way to any spontaneous reaction. Although she was anxious, distressed, perhaps scared, she retained sufficient self-control to consider her words. Finally, with averted eyes, she asked: 'Are you saying they murdered her?'

'No, I don't know one way or the other, but at the moment it seems that she could well have died a natural death.'

Esther was frowning. 'Then why — ?' But she broke off without completing her sentence.

Bleached light from a tall window filled the room and explored its shabbiness: the threadbare carpet, the worn upholstery, the dusty cornices and discoloured walls.

Esther smoothed the folds of her dress over her bony knees. Wycliffe made an effort to ease the tension. 'I wonder if you would tell me something about the Rules and the Clemos — about the two families and how they are related.'

She looked up at him with suspicious eyes but his expression, mild and receptive, reassured her. 'It's not complicated. James Clemo's mother, Elinor, who died last week, was a Rule. One of her brothers, Gordon, married Jane, his first cousin, and they rented Tregelles from the Clemos.'

'And Agnes was a sister?'

'Yes, there were two girls and two boys. The two boys, Henry and Gordon, are both dead. Agnes kept house for Henry until he died, then she moved in with her sister-in-law at Tregelles.'

Esther was relaxing. An attentive listener is better than any amount of diazepam.

Wycliffe allowed a comfortable measure of silence before asking: 'Was there money in the Rule family?'

'Not much. Their father kept a general store in the village; but after the war Henry made money in antiques.'

'What happened to his money?'

'I reckon he gambled away most of it, but Agnes looked after him for nearly forty years, so I suppose what was left came to her.' She broke off. 'You *do* think she was murdered! That's what this is all about!' She was accusing.

'No, I've told you the truth. At the moment I've no reason to think that Agnes was murdered.'

But Esther was unconvinced. 'Anyway it's nothing to do with me — nothing! The Rules are no concern of mine now, thank God!'

'*Now*?'

She flushed, the deep colour spread upwards from her neck to her pale cheeks. 'I used to work for them.'

'Before you came to live here?'

'When I was fifteen. You left school at fifteen then — at least people like me did.'

'You were adopted by the Clemos?'

'That's what it amounted to.'

'The Rules were unkind to you?'

She shifted uneasily. 'There's something queer about that family — they're twisted, all of them!'

'But Elinor Clemo was a Rule before she married, surely?'

A sidelong glance. 'And she took me in so I should be grateful. Is that what you're saying? You can believe me she did it for her own ends. Anyway, it's all over now and that's all I'm going to say. It's my business and it's staying that way.'

'Who were your real parents?'

She shrugged her thin shoulders but did not answer.

'You are worried about Hilda?'

'Of course I'm worried! I brought her up from the age of four — after her mother died.'

69

'Can you make any suggestion at all as to what might have happened to her?'

She was silent for some time but he saw her eyes redden and fill with tears. In a hoarse voice she said: 'I don't know what could have happened to her; I wish to God I did! All I know is I wish you could find her — alive if possible, but find her! It's not knowing!'

After a pause she added: 'And you should keep the Rules locked up for their own good.'

'What does that mean?'

'Nothing. They aren't safe loose.'

Chapter Five

Tuesday afternoon

'Charles! I can't help it if it takes time to thaw her out. As far as I can see there are no external injuries, but even that isn't certain at this stage. Did you read about the trouble the Russians took unfreezing the couple dug out of their permafrost?'

'I'm not interested in the Russians or their permafrost; I want to know how that woman died.'

'Then, my friend, you'll have to wait. What do you expect me to do? Set to with a blowtorch? I need relatively undamaged material. God knows how far putrefaction had gone before the freezing process became effective. I can't afford to risk further tissue breakdown through a too rapid thaw, just because you're in a hurry, Charles.'

But there was a placatory last word: 'Anyway, I'll try to have something for you tomorrow.'

So much for Dr Franks.

The pathologist's call was followed almost at once by one from John Scales: 'About this fellow, Innes, sir. He's quite well known in academic circles as an art historian but he's outside the establishment. He took a fine arts degree, followed by three or four years at the V & A, but after that he dropped out of the academic rat race. Now he tops up his rice bowl by contributing articles to glossy magazines and by lecturing on the extra-mural circuit.'

'Background?'

'Father has a prosperous West End business in Oriental antiques, import–export as well as retail business; lives in St

John's Wood, motor cruiser on the Hamble. There's a rumour that, for some reason, Tristan has been cut off without the proverbial shilling.'

The rain had stopped and the sun was shining; the tiers of little terraced houses on the other side of the harbour were a dazzling patchwork of colour under the inky-blackness of a retreating cloud. The time by the clock on the plywood partition was 15.05, or, in translation, five minutes past three in the afternoon.

Detective Sergeant Lucy Lane had arrived to join the team, and it said something for her tenacity and resource over three years that Wycliffe was glad, even a little relieved, to see her. Still under thirty; dark hair and eyes, and 36-24-36 — a package with no chance of an unruffled reception by the squad. Another forty pounds or an incipient moustache would have helped; as it was she had fended off critics and repelled would-be boarders with hard work and a capacity for stinging repartee.

Wycliffe said: 'Any news of the Rules?'

'Still at subdivision making their statements, with Curnow as nursemaid.'

'I don't want them detained, at least not until we've had a report from Franks.'

Kersey nodded. 'I know, I had a word with Jim Nicolls; they'll be released pending further enquiries.' He hesitated, then went on: 'You don't think you're taking a bit of a chance?'

'We'll see. Find out when they're due to arrive home. We'll have a man keeping obo overnight. There's no one place from where he could see all that might go on, so he'll have to use his wits and move about a bit. Observation only; no interference without radio clearance except in emergency.'

Kersey made a note.

Lucy Lane tried to get the broader picture: 'Do we assume, sir, that there is a connection between the girl's disappearance and the old lady in the freezer?'

Women have a knack of asking the crunch question.

Wycliffe played with a ball-point, making a complex pattern of dots on a scribbling pad, and evading a direct answer. 'On Friday afternoon Elinor Clemo was buried. According to the Rules, her sister, Agnes, had died of heart failure that morning. On Saturday morning, Hilda Clemo — granddaughter to Elinor, and great-niece to Agnes — is told that she's pregnant. That afternoon Hilda disappears, last seen on her way home over the Rules' fields. As a tailpiece, we find Agnes's body in the freezer.'

Kersey grimaced. 'Put like that it seems rather much for one family in two days.'

Lucy Lane said: 'It sounds like the synopsis of a Buñuel film.'

Kersey looked at her, poker-faced. 'What sort of films did he make? Westerns? What we should be asking is whether there's money behind it.'

Wycliffe agreed. 'That's one of the things we have to find out.'

Lucy Lane was wearing that special frown that made her look like a pensive schoolgirl in need of a pen to suck. 'For practical purposes are we assuming that the girl has been murdered?'

Kersey, who treasured a rag-bag of lost causes like real bread, hanging, and paying cash, had never wholly resigned himself to working with women in the serious crimes squad. Traffic, non-violent juveniles, the victim's angle on rape, liaison with social services — all these, and more, he willingly conceded to the woman's sphere, but there were limits, and occasionally the cloven hoof showed.

'With no body, with not a shred of evidence to suggest that she is dead, and with no known motive for anyone to kill her, I find it hard to see how we can assume, even tactically, that she has been murdered.'

Wycliffe was joining his dots together to make a passable drawing of a bird in flight. 'I don't think we should jump to any conclusions until we can see some sort of pattern. All the same, I can't help being pessimistic about the girl. If she intended to leave home, would she have gone off with the boy on a boat trip? Would she have started out in jeans and a sweat-shirt, taking nothing with her? But assuming she had reasons for doing both these things, would she then have left the boat at the Haven and struck out across the fields towards home? We know now that's what she did.

'For the moment we need to follow two lines: get all we can on the girl; on her family, and her associates outside the family. I've a feeling that she used Ralph Martin; that there's someone else in the background who, for some reason, she decided to shield. I want you, Lucy, to get more insight into the family — I'm interested in the son-in-law, Bertie, who seems a bit nebulous so far.'

'You want me to talk to him, sir?'

'I think you should make his acquaintance. And have a word with others employed on the site, try to get their view of the family. There must be quite a few seasonal and part-time workers. Do we have anything on Bertie in Rowse's notes?'

Kersey reached for the file and flipped the pages. 'Not much. He married Alice and came to work here in 1983. Before that he was employed for several years by Lovell and Delbos, the Exeter auctioneers.'

'Sounds all right, but make discreet enquiries into background and present activities. Get one of our chaps to pay a call on Lovell and Delbos to find out what his job was and why he left. Meanwhile, Lucy, go and talk to him.

'Incidentally, where was he on Saturday afternoon when the girl disappeared?'

Lucy checked the file of routine interviews. 'He made a statement to one of Inspector Rowse's men . . . Here it is: "On Saturday afternoon I drove the Land Rover to the garage at Highlanes to have the towbar welded . . ."' Lucy scanned the typescript: 'He arrived there at about four and left at five-thirty; he did not stay in the garage the whole time but went for a stroll . . . Saw nobody that he remembers . . . He arrived back at the caravan park at quarter to six and spent some time tinkering in the implements shed . . . Arrived at the house just before seven, in time for the evening meal.'

'And this garage, where is it?'

'On the Gorran road, within half a mile of the farm.'

Wycliffe nodded. 'Wide open. The Rules are the same. Innes admits meeting and talking to the girl at a little before five . . . What about the Moyles? Four sons and no father, that's it, isn't it?'

Again Lucy turned the pages of the file. 'As I remember they were all four off on a trip on Saturday afternoon . . . Yes, here we are — Exeter, stock-car racing. Inspector Rowse checked that out. They didn't get back until nine in the evening.'

Wycliffe nodded. 'Of course there's nothing to say that the girl's assailant, if there was one, is known to us, but everything points that way. I mean, this doesn't look like a pick-up and rape, there's nothing to suggest that she was on the highway. Although it takes up a lot of man-hours we must push on with enquiries among males within as wide a radius as we can manage: "Where were you on Saturday afternoon? Did you see . . .?" Et cetera.'

Kersey said: 'We're doing all we can on those lines, sir.'

'Right! Now, in connection with the old woman's death, I want you to look at the inheritance angle. Granny Clemo, née Rule, died last week, and her sister, Agnes, was already dead or died soon afterwards. There must be a lawyer somewhere in the business. Find out from Alice Harvey, she'll know. We've enough evidence to suggest that there's been at least one serious crime, so you should be able to turn the screw if necessary.'

Kersey said: 'Presumably you're staying on the case now, sir?'

'If I can find somewhere to sleep.'

'There's a vacancy where I am and it's not bad, especially if you're allowed to eat the breakfast.'

'All right, see if you can fix it.'

'You don't look a bit like a cop to me.'

'Your experience is probably limited, Mr Harvey.'

They were at the top end of the caravan park, in a building adjoining the implements shed, where would-be swimmers, tennis players and golfers paid their fees, and collected whatever gear they needed in return for a deposit.

'I'm supposed to be the site manager,' Bertie said. 'In fact, I'm a dogsbody in this place. I do anything from cleaning the loos or cutting the grass, to binding the wounds and consoling the mothers of small brats who fall out of trees or tumble off the climbing-frame. In a crisis I've even been drafted in to chat up the VAT man.' He grinned at her. 'Little friend of all the world: that's me.'

Lucy Lane did not quite know what to make of him. He had charm, and knew it, but she sensed an underlying seriousness which might be worth exploring.

'I want to talk to you about Hilda.'

'About Hilda.' He was immediately solemn. 'Hilda was special.'

'*Was*?'

'You don't imagine that she's still alive, do you?'

'In the absence of evidence to the contrary we have to assume that she is. But perhaps you know something which we don't.'

The dark eyes were on her. 'Now, however you look, you sound just like a policeman, and not a very bright one at that. No, I don't know anything about what has happened to Hilda.'

'All right. You said that she was special; will you enlarge on that?'

'Yes. She was very intelligent, she knew precisely what she wanted, she knew how to use people, and, unlike most young people, she knew better than to let her emotions get in the way.'

'But she was pregnant.'

'That did surprise me. I'll guarantee one thing, that it wasn't the young clodhopper on the boats who got her that way. The seduction of Hilda would have required finesse, a skilful wooing of mind and spirit as well as of the flesh. A task for a man of discretion and experience.'

'Yourself, for example?'

'I take your point; fresher fruit from the same tree. I must confess that I was tempted but, like Hilda, I'm a realist and the situation would have become altogether too messy for my liking.'

'So?'

'So nothing as far as I'm concerned. I can't help you.'

A couple, the man in trunks, the girl in a bikini, came to the window to collect a token for the pool.

Bertie Harvey was a man to be reckoned with. If his position was really one of general dogsbody it was unlikely that he accepted it as meekly as he pretended. He was attractive to women; Lucy Lane was aware of the attraction, though she told herself that he was not — repeat not — a man to be married to. But Alice Clemo had married him.

When he had dealt with his customers she said: 'You've got some very definite opinions about Hilda; presumably you know her well.'

'I've lived in the same house with her for five years and we've talked quite a bit.'

'About what?'

'Oh, cabbages and kings.'

'I see. And whether pigs have wings.'

He smiled. 'A Carroll addict?'

'I'm afraid so.'

'Me too. And Hilda caught it off me.'

Damn the man! 'Getting back to the point: did Hilda confide in you at all?'

'I don't think Hilda confided in anybody. She would talk freely enough for just as long as you remembered the mask.'

'The mask?'

'Doesn't everybody wear one? Of course most people let you have a peek behind now and then — not Hilda; if you even tried, it was end of conversation.'

Lucy Lane felt vulnerable — which was absurd. 'Did you and Hilda discuss anything in particular? I mean, in recent months or weeks did it seem to you that she had anything on her mind that troubled her?'

'Nothing that troubled her particularly; we talked about anything and everything.'

It was leading nowhere; she was bungling a potentially important interview. 'Do you know Jane Rule?'

'The Red Queen.'

'Why do you call her that?'

'Because, poor soul, she's always running to stay where she is. I feel sorry for her, and the Clemos don't help.'

'Do you see others of your acquaintance as Alice characters?'

Harvey laughed. 'Some. My father-in-law, for instance, he's an obvious King of Hearts: officious, a bit bumbling, but really quite likeable.'

'And you, yourself?'

'Oh, I'm the Knave, definitely. I stole the tarts — perhaps that should be singular but then it would sound rude and we should never be rude, should we?' A pause and he went on: 'Of course I could be Humpty Dumpty.'

'Why Humpty Dumpty?'

'Well, poor chap, he was balanced on a wall, wasn't he? And his only way off was to fall.' He was looking at her, not smiling, but with a speculative gaze. 'If it's of any interest, I see you, at this moment, as Alice — not quite sure which side of the looking glass she is.'

Bastard! But she did not say it aloud.

Bertie had more customers, four of them, wanting to play golf, and while he was dealing with them Lucy took stock of the place. The room they were in was provided with racks for storing clubs, racquets, skateboards, and other impedimenta for the various diversions available to the paying customer. There were also displays of sweat-shirts, caps and sunglasses for sale.

A door led off to an office and, beyond that, there was another room which, to Lucy's surprise, was fitted up as a darkroom with shutters to draw across the window, and an array of equipment for processing and enlarging. On a bench, in polythene envelopes, with name-tags and prices attached, were photographs awaiting collection.

'So you're a photographer — also like Lewis Carroll.'

'I enjoy it and it's another way of turning an honest penny.' Bertie was standing in the doorway watching her. 'They come here with two or three hundred quid's worth of camera strapped around their necks, then pay me to take photographs of their kids with my old Praktica that mother gave me when I was eighteen. To coin a phrase: "There's now't so queer as folk!"'

Kersey had no difficulty in running Agnes Rule's lawyer to earth. Everybody knew Hector Penrose who had acted for the Rules and the Clemos through the better part of three generations. Now, officially retired, he lived in a low, white house, high above the village, on the north side of the harbour and overlooking the bay.

Kersey was shown into an untidy room with a bow-window looking, inevitably, over the bay. Sky and sea seemed unnaturally blue after the rain, the gulls whiter, the sun brighter. Penrose was seated at a large desk with several pages from a loose-leaf stamp album spread in front of him. He brandished a hand-lens, waving Kersey to a seat. There was a book-rack of catalogues on the desk, a scattering of philatelic journals, other tools of the trade, and a sleeping tabby cat.

'Inspector Kersey.' The old man looked at him critically. 'Not, I think, of the Cornish Kerseys.'

'I'm told that my people came originally from Suffolk.'

Penrose nodded. 'As I thought. Well, we can't all be of God's chosen.' He chuckled. 'As long as we show proper humility . . .'

'I've been told, sir, that you act for the Rule family.'

'Actually I retired several years ago but a few of my old clients who dislike change have stayed with me. My successors in the practice are tolerant and they do all the chores.'

He examined a couple of loose stamps through his hand-lens and muttered unintelligibly. 'You are not interested in stamps, Mr Kersey? No, of course not — pity! As far as the Rules are concerned I gather that Jane is in some difficulty over the discovery of her sister-in-law's body in her freezer. Obviously I can't comment on that, so what can I do for you?'

He was plump and pink with curly white hair which glistened in the sunlight.

'Some background on the family would be helpful, sir.'

'But you can pick that up from local gossip.'

'More painfully and less reliably, sir.'

The old man laughed. 'Well, there's little enough to tell. John Henry Rule had a general store in the village, worked hard all his life, and made very little. He had two sons: Henry and Gordon — ' He broke off. 'Dear me! I can't make up my mind if this one-cent is from the retouched die or not . . .

'Anyway, Henry went to work for an antique dealer in Plymouth and eventually took over the business. Gordon married your Jane and they rented Tregelles from the Clemos. The two brothers had two sisters: one, Elinor, married a Clemo

79

— it was through her that Gordon got the tenancy at Tregelles. The other sister, Agnes, spent most of her life looking after brother Henry, and when he died she went to live with her sister-in-law at Tregelles. There's the background you asked for, Mr Kersey.'

The lawyer was making a close comparison of the two stamps under a light fitted with some sort of filter. 'The colours are different too . . . If that's carmine, I'm a Dutchman.'

Kersey said: 'Wasn't it Henry who made the money, sir?'

A sidelong glance. 'What money? I said nothing about money. But you're quite right. People who'd lined their pockets in the war and were looking for an inflation-proof investment went in for antiques. Henry found them the right antiques and made a lot of money.'

'What happened to it? The money, I mean.'

Penrose made a derogatory sound. 'I'll have nothing to do with modern stamps — nothing since the last war. Too many damned commemoratives — a racket! Even our lot have cashed in on it.'

'Henry's money, sir — what happened to it?'

'He spent most of it, gambled it away on horses with two wooden legs apiece. When he died everything was left, in trust, to Agnes for life. The house was too big for her, so it was let, and she moved in with Jane at Tregelles.'

'What happens now?'

'Ah! I'm not sure that I can go that far, Mr Kersey.' He was comparing watermarks on his two stamps. 'I remember the excitement there was when they issued special stamps for the Wembley Exhibition of 1924. I was only a boy at the time. And the Postal Union Congress issue of 1929 — marvellous! Now the damn things rain down like confetti.'

'But Agnes Rule is dead, sir.'

'Yes, and in very peculiar circumstances.' He turned away from his stamps with reluctance. 'I suppose it's my duty to assist you. Well, according to the will, if Elinor survived Agnes, everything came to her.'

'And if Agnes survived Elinor?'

'Then the trust was automatically wound up and Agnes became the unconditional legatee.'

'One more question, sir — Agnes's will, if she made one . . .'

The old man sighed. 'In for a penny . . . Agnes did make a will and in it she left everything to Jane.'

'Hence the freezer.'

'I didn't hear that, Inspector.'

Penrose became thoughtful, tapping on the desk with a forceps he happened to be holding, and disturbing the cat. 'Before you jump to any conclusions, Mr Kersey, bear in mind that we are not talking about a large estate — Henry's house is in a part of the city which has gone down hill very badly in recent years; there's some furniture stored at Tregelles, and a small amount of money in shares. Of course when Henry made his will he expected to die a rich man.'

Kersey stood up. 'Thank you very much for your help, sir.'

'You should take up philately, Inspector, it teaches you patience.'

Chapter Six

Tuesday afternoon (continued)

'Hilda is a brilliant pupil; the astonishing thing is that she rarely displays any apparent interest . . .'

'She takes no part in the corporate life of the school outside the classroom — no games, no drama, no choir . . .'

'Her attitude to the staff is one of indifference . . . Teaching her is unrewarding in the sense that one is treated like a reference book — there is no real contact . . .'

'Her attitude to the boys is mildly contemptuous . . . She became friendly with a girl from Gorran but it didn't last. Hilda is a loner . . .'

'Ralph Martin? Yes, I know him; he was at the school. Not bright, but a pleasant lad . . . I can't believe that Hilda . . . She must be playing with him; she can be very cruel.'

'There must be something which makes her tick but I've never discovered what it is.'

Wycliffe was briefing himself on reports of interviews and on notes made by the interviewing officers. The most illuminating comments on the girl had come from her teachers.

'The girl' — Since the previous afternoon when he had opened the file and seen the face of the missing girl looking up at him she had rarely been out of his mind. He found it impossible to treat the case like any other, it had assumed the aspects of a crusade — not that he had any expectation of finding her alive.

Hilda was dead.

Wycliffe was in a cubby-hole, part of the Incident Van reserved for the officer in charge. Next door, in a larger cubicle, a couple of typewriters were clacking away, contributing to the great edifice of paper which is always the most tangible outcome of any inquiry. Soon he would take over an empty shop premises which Shaw had negotiated. It was on the northern quay, close to the harbour office; the shop, and two rooms over. Luxury! They would be equipped from central stores: the typewriters would be electronic, there would be VDU screens, a computer terminal, and a link with the police communications network. The bureaucracy of crime.

The window of his present cell was fitted with frosted glass, presumably to shield the populace from the spectacle of a police chief sucking the end of his ball-point; but Wycliffe found it claustrophobic and, when he could stand it no longer, he left the van and strolled along the quay like a tourist.

The whole village had a newly washed look after the rain; the air was fresher, perhaps with a hint of autumn; it was the first day of September. With the approach of the school term visitors with children of school age would soon be gone from the streets; for another month there would be coachloads of the middle-aged and elderly to keep the shops and cafés happy, then the village would revert to its quieter more inward-looking way of life — the norm for seven or eight months of the year.

This girl — this pregnant girl . . . Why was he so certain that she was dead? Why was he sure that she had been murdered? Was there any connection between her disappearance and the old woman in the freezer? If only he could marshall the facts and reason from them; but his mind, as always, was a play-ground for remembered phrases, pictures, ideas, fancies, over which he exercised only a tenuous control. Although he had read Koestler and Storr on creativity, he still had an uncomfortable feeling that the thought processes of intelligent people should be organized in a series of logical deductive steps like a Euclidean proof.

He was on his way to the caravan park to talk to Alice Harvey and he found her alone in Reception. Cars were entering and leaving the site, people were in and out of the shop and café, but Reception was quiet.

'Chief Superintendent Wycliffe . . . You, I believe, are Mrs Harvey, Hilda's sister . . .'

'Have you any news?'

'I'm sorry, no.'

'Do you mind if we talk here? There is no one to relieve me at the moment.'

She found him a chair which she placed by her desk. She was pale, and her eyes were darkened by tiredness. The family resemblance to the girl in the photograph was unmistakable but Alice was putting on weight and already she was beginning to pout. Another neatly packaged bundle of frustrations, product of the Ad-world.

She offered him a cigarette which he refused. 'Do you mind if I do? It keeps me going.' A wan smile, self-conscious. She lit a cigarette with uncertain hands.

He expressed sympathy. 'All this on top of your grandmother's death.'

Her eyes had a faraway look. 'Yes, we buried Granny on Friday and it seems an age since then.'

'Had she been ill for long?'

'Nearly three months — following a stroke.' She changed the subject abruptly: 'You think Hilda is dead, don't you?'

'Do you think she left home of her own accord?'

'I'm quite sure she didn't!' The words seem to spill out. A moment of hesitation, then: 'Do you still suspect Ralph Martin?'

'Why do you ask?'

She was impatient with evasion and snapped out her reply: 'He's been interviewed three times by the police, hasn't he?'

'Because by his own admission he was among the last to see your sister, and because his account of the circumstances was far from straightforward.'

She looked around for an ashtray and, failing to find one, tapped ash into a potted plant. 'Ralph wouldn't hurt anybody, least of all Hilda.'

'Do you have any idea who might have harmed her?'

She shied away from that. 'Of course not! How could I?'

He said nothing but his steady, brooding gaze disturbed her and, in the end, it was she who broke the silence. In preparation she slid her chair back from the desk and swivelled round as though to confront him. 'I suppose you think Hilda was innocent, with no previous sexual experience?'

'Is that what you believe?'

'I don't think that Ralph Martin was the only one . . . It sounds unfeeling to talk like this now but it could have something to do with whatever happened.' An irritable gesture, then: 'Of course my father wouldn't believe anything of the kind, it would be useless to talk to him.'

She was watching Wycliffe through a haze of cigarette smoke and, after an uneasy pause, she burst out: 'Hilda is a very strange girl, Mr Wycliffe. I can't quite explain, but she seems to treat people as if . . . as if they were white mice, or something . . . Wouldn't it be interesting to try this, or that? I don't think she ever put herself in anyone else's shoes.'

She coloured. 'This must sound dreadful to you but I think you should know.'

'You think she was using Ralph Martin to experiment?'

'I don't know but it seems likely to me.' She turned on her chair. 'Ralph is the sort of boy who lays himself open for it.'

The door opened and James Clemo came in. He stood, looking from one to the other. 'What's going on?' His arms hung loose but his fists were clenched and he pivoted on the balls of his feet in a boxer's stance.

Alice said: 'My father.'

Wycliffe introduced himself. 'I've taken over the investigation into your daughter's disappearance. Let me say — '

'My daughter has been raped and murdered; don't play the word game with me, mister! What will you do with him when you catch him?'

Wycliffe's answer was low key, matter of fact: 'My job is to investigate the circumstances of her disappearance, Mr Clemo. If it turns out that she has been harmed and someone is arrested and charged with an offence, it will be up to the courts to decide what happens after that.'

Clemo was watching the superintendent, his grey eyes unwavering. 'And if they find him guilty; what will they do with him? Will they hang him?'

Wycliffe's manner did not change. 'I'm sure you know that there is no capital punishment in this country, Mr Clemo.'

Clemo raised his arms. 'So why bother?'

Wycliffe sympathized with the man's despair but said nothing. It was Alice who spoke: 'You're doing no good, father.'

Clemo turned on her in anger but, face to face with his daughter, it seemed that his aggression vanished, leaving him limp and listless. After a while he said in a low voice: 'No, you're quite right, Alice. I'm doing no good at all — and neither is he. Hilda is dead and we're wasting our time.'

He went out as he had come, closing the door behind him.

Alice said: 'You see how things are?' It was a plea.

'Who is Esther? How did she come into the family?'

'Esther?' She was momentarily put off by the abrupt change of subject but she collected her wits. 'Esther was adopted by my grandparents as a girl of sixteen.' A vague gesture. 'Don't ask me why, I don't know; I was only six when she came and it is a subject never talked about. Anyway, when mother died Esther took over the running of the house and she's been doing it ever since. I was fifteen and Hilda was four then.'

'But who is she? Who were her parents?'

A brief hesitation. 'You must ask her that.'

Wycliffe was casting around, trying to trigger any revealing response, and he tried again: 'I understand that Hilda doesn't visit her Rule relations at Tregelles.'

'None of us does. Hilda used to go there until about a year ago when Agnes started to go queer in the head. They seemed to get on, but nobody gets on with Jane. The truth is there's been friction for a long time. Granny persuaded grandfather to let her brother, Gordon, rent Tregelles. That worked more or less until Gordon died, but since then the farm has gone downhill, it's turning into a wilderness and the rent is laughable for these days. Now that Granny's gone I hope father will do something about it.'

These were things Wycliffe understood; his father had been a small-time tenant farmer and he had been brought up in the narrow world of family feuds, squabbles over land, and the conflicting interests of landlord and tenant.

With seeming irrelevance, Alice said: 'You think Agnes was murdered, don't you?'

'I don't think anything. We shan't know until I have the pathologist's report. Jane Rule says she died of a heart attack last Friday morning, the day of your grandmother's funeral.'

'But they didn't send for a doctor, they put her in the freezer!' Alice shuddered and seemed genuinely distressed. 'It's horrible! I can't take it in. Last Friday we seemed to be a family like any other; now — soon, people will read about us in the newspapers and they'll think we are — I don't know — grotesque!' She was trembling.

A young girl came into the office and stood irresolute on seeing Wycliffe. 'I'm sorry I'm a bit late . . .'

Alice regained her control. 'My relief. We can go into the house now if you want to.'

'Yes, I would like to see your sister's room.'

'Her room? Two policemen went through her things yesterday but of course you can see it.'

They walked up the drive together and he followed her into the hall and up the stairs. Everywhere there were signs of neglect: worn carpets, woodwork in need of paint, and the patterns on the wallpapers had merged into a general drabness. A long passage on the first floor divided the house almost into two, with a window at one end and a room at the other. Hilda's was the end room and it came as a pleasant surprise.

The window overlooked a little patch of woodland which separated the house from the road. The room might have belonged to a fairly prosperous young student almost anywhere: light, functional furniture from Habitat; shelves for books, and a music centre . . . The pictures were semi-abstract and vaguely erotic, with a suggestion of improbably entangled limbs. The desk stood beneath the window.

Alice said: 'I expect you know that she's working for her A–levels and the school says she should get an Oxford award.'

'What subjects?'

'English Literature, French, English and European History — a very traditional menu for a bright girl but she chose it herself.'

Wycliffe looked about him; he opened drawers and cupboards at random, picked up books and put them down again. When he looked in the wardrobe Alice said: 'At least she didn't go mad on clothes like most girls.'

The books were largely concerned with her school work but there was a spread of paperbacks, from foreign classics (mainly French) to Le Carré and other writers of intelligent spy fiction. Odd taste for a girl, Wycliffe thought, male chauvinist that he was. Conspicuous among the books because of its twelve hundred pages: *The Works of Lewis Carroll*; Wycliffe picked up the book and opened it. The flyleaf was inscribed: 'To Hilda on her thirteenth birthday with love from the Knave.'

'My husband — Bertie,' Alice said.

He replaced the book. Alice stood as though waiting for some comment or question and when none came, she added: 'He's very fond of Hilda.' Toneless.

'Am I intended to read something into that?'

She looked away. 'Bertie can be very charming when he wants to.'

'It wouldn't be the first time that a husband has been attracted to a young sister-in-law.'

She walked to the window. 'I don't know anything.'

'But you suspect. What, exactly?'

She turned on him, suddenly angry. 'Do you expect me to spell it out? To put all our dirty linen on the line? The fact is I can't really believe that Bertie was having sex with Hilda. He isn't all that interested beyond the titillation stage. If you want it plainer, he's all right with a woman until she takes her pants off.'

He was looking through the records and cassettes all neatly stored in racks and it was as though he had not heard her outburst. 'It looks as though pop has been overtaken by the classical here.'

'What? Oh, yes.' She seemed relieved, perhaps grateful. 'Until a few months ago we were under siege from pop, now it's more likely to be a Bach prelude or a Mozart quintet.'

'What inspired the change?'

'I don't know. Girls go through phases. At about the same time she went over to high fibre and fruit juice.'

Wycliffe was idly turning the pages of one of Hilda's school files. 'Does she support any causes?'

'Causes?'

'Anti-nuclear, anti-pollution, anti-vivisection; save seals, whales, badgers and children.'

Alice smiled. 'Do you know I've never even thought of Hilda in connection with anything of that sort.'

'So she doesn't.'

'No. Hilda reacts to the world only as it directly affects her.'

'Do you know the Inneses at Tregelles Cottage?'

She was becoming accustomed to his abrupt changes of subject. 'They're our tenants. That bungalow was originally built for mother and father when they married but they changed their minds and lived here. Anyway, what about the Inneses?'

'Did you know that Hilda has been a fairly frequent visitor there for several months past?'

'No, I didn't know that. Are you saying that she might have gone there on Saturday afternoon?'

'Innes met her on the field path between the Haven and the farm at about five on Saturday afternoon. She told him she was on her way home. What do you know about him?'

Alice was thoughtful. 'Not a lot. I've heard that his father deals in oriental stuff and that he's got a plush showroom in the West End. Innes is a lecturer and I think he writes articles for up-market magazines. His wife is a cripple.'

'Any scandal?'

'That depends on what you mean by scandal. They owe us money for rent and I hear they're in debt elsewhere. I gather his relations with his father are not all that good.'

Wycliffe said: 'I've seen all I wanted to see here, thank you, but I would like a quick look at the other rooms.'

89

'The other rooms?' She was surprised.

'You object?'

'Why should I? It just seemed odd.'

He led the way into the passage and stopped by the first door.

'That's my room.' She pushed open the door and stood aside. 'You must take it as you find it.' There was a double bed made up for one; a built-in wardrobe, a dressing-table, and a wash-basin. A few books shared a shelf by the bed with a clock–radio. The carpet had not seen a vacuum cleaner for a long time.

He was shown the other bedrooms but only two were of real interest and each of these came as a surprise.

Bertie Harvey slept in a large room with a single bed, more of a study than a bedroom. There was a desk, a filing cabinet, and half of one wall was taken up with bookshelves. The books were about equally divided between nineteenth-century biographies and a specialized collection of works by and about Lewis Carroll, including the mathematical publications under his own name: Charles Dodgson.

Alice said: 'It's an obsession. I think he married me because my name was Alice. He's writing a book called *Alice Now*, and the latest is that he's applied for a place on the next *Mastermind* series on TV with the life and works of Lewis Carroll as his specialist subject.'

'Are the photographs his?'

Wherever there was an available piece of wall there were photographs of children — mainly girls.

'Don't you remember? Lewis Carroll was a pioneer photo-grapher and his subjects were usually young girls. I think Peter was a great disappointment to Bertie. Before Peter was born he used to quote Lewis Carroll: "I like all children except boys." He doesn't say that now but I don't think he's changed.'

Wycliffe hesitated. 'Do you think it's sexual?' It was a stupid question but he wanted to prime the pump.

'I suppose it is, but that doesn't mean that I think Bertie molests little girls. I don't suppose Carroll did either, though there would probably have been less fuss in his day if he had.'

She was looking round the room with a half-smile on her lips. 'In some ways Bertie is still a child himself; that's the trouble . . . Anyway, it's better like this — separate rooms, I mean.'

They crossed the passage. 'This is Esther's.'

The other room he had most wanted to see, and it was unexpected. Immediately opposite the door, on the wall by the window, was a highly ornate plaster statue of the Virgin and, over the bed, a crucifix.

'I can see that you're surprised. She became a Catholic shortly after my mother died — thirteen years ago . . . And you know what they say about converts.'

There was a missal on the bedside table and shelves of religious works, mainly lives of the saints.

He'd had enough to be going on with. His mind had been offered a succession of facts, images, phrases, hints and evasions which he would store away for later rumination. He had been given glimpses of the missing girl in her home, and revealing sketches of her as seen through her sister's eyes. He had seen something of the sombre neglected house, and he had been in the little room which the girl had made her own, as different from the rest of the house as she could contrive.

He had met James Clemo.

'Well, thank you for being so patient and helpful, Mrs Harvey. I shall be back from time to time, but if you want to get in touch don't hesitate to ring the Incident Van on the quay.'

Alice followed him down the stairs. On the front steps she said: 'Don't take too much notice of me. I'm not myself.'

Wycliffe walked back to the Incident Van. He felt frustrated, like a child grasping at soap bubbles. He was sure that the key to much of what had happened lay in the character of the girl, but what he had seen and heard gave him no coherent picture and he was back with her teacher's comment: 'There must be something which makes her tick but I've never discovered what it is.'

In the Incident Van Lucy Lane was typing her report, the only officer on the strength without an addiction to eraser fluid.

'Well?'

'I've had a difficult afternoon, sir. I've completely failed to make anything of Harvey.'

'Let's hear it.'

Lucy Lane told her story, and finished: 'He has a certain zany charm which is obviously superficial, but you realize that to bring it off at all requires intelligence. If he's a villain it's going to take us all our time to pin him down.'

'Did you get round to talking to anybody else?'

'I went to see the Moyles. Inspector Rowse left us a list of people employed full-time and part-time in the park. Among them are two of the Moyle family who live not far from the Rules: a girl, Debbie, who works evenings in the shop; and a boy, Jeff, who's a full-time handyman. I caught Debbie at home with her mother.'

Lucy Lane swivelled round on her chair to face him. 'The inside of that house is a revelation! You can't make up your mind whether you're in a kitchen or a run-down motor repair shop. Oily bits and pieces of cars are mixed up with the dirty dishes and the vegetables for tonight's meal. Mrs Moyle, with swollen legs and wearing carpet slippers, pads about doing this and that, serenely content. Debbie is a pretty girl of about twenty-two. Wearing a bra and pants, she was ironing shirts for the boys and those shirts looked clean, though God knows how they managed it.'

Lucy could be relied on to sketch in background and that pleased Wycliffe; it was the next best thing to having been there himself.

'Debbie likes working for the Clemos; the pay is quite good and they get a bonus at the end of the season. James's bark scares nobody and she finds Alice easy to get on with. She's not so sure about Bertie; neither, it seems, are the others. The general complaint about him is that nobody knows where they are with him. He can be very sarcastic and he says things they don't know how to take. I can believe that! He also takes photographs of little girls and, according to Debbie, we all know what that means.'

'Anything on the Rules?'

'I was coming to that, sir. The Rules are definitely unpopular with the Moyles. Mother had a few things to say about them; according to her, they come from bad stock: Jane, Clifford, Agnes, even Granny Clemo who died last week — she was a Rule before she married.'

'Any examples?'

'Oh, yes. Clifford is a half-wit, his father was peculiar — "And look at Jane! There's got to be something wrong with a woman who puts her sister-in-law's body in the freezer, whether she died natural or no!" I couldn't argue with that, and when I pointed out that Jane was only a Rule by marriage, she said that was all I knew; that, in fact, Jane was her husband's first cousin.'

Wycliffe remembered the 'tainted' families from his own childhood. Rustic genetics. 'Anything else?'

'Yes, but I'm not sure whether it means anything. Debbie says that twice in the past few months she's seen Bertie with the site Land Rover down beside the farmhouse, loading pieces of furniture.'

'Jane, selling off Agnes's heirlooms?'

'That's what the Moyles think. It interested me because Bertie professed kindly feelings towards Jane.'

'See what you can find out.'

'Anything else for me, sir?'

'Yes. I've just come from the Clemo's place; I want you to spend some time in Hilda's room, going through everything you can find.'

'Shall I be looking for anything in particular?'

A thin smile. 'Only for the real Hilda Clemo.'

Wycliffe and Kersey lingered over their coffee in the hotel dining-room, feeling pleasantly lethargic.

The hotel was on rising ground, virtually a cliff-top, to the west of the village, overlooking — almost overhanging — the harbour. From the dining-room windows the lights along the waterfront and quays defined the dark pools of the inner and outer harbours, and the lighthouse flashed at the tip of the southern arm.

'I think I shall go for a walk.'

It was a ritual after his evening meal, whenever he was away from home. Kersey knew better than to offer his company. He said: 'I thought of going for a drink at The Seiners later on.'

'I might see you there in about an hour.'

It was a windless night, cloudless too. Wycliffe was on his way down the steep, narrow, and sinuous road to the village; on one side, houses; on the other, a low wall and a long drop.

What Henry Rule had to leave might not have seemed much to his lawyer, but viewed from that kitchen at Tregelles Farm it probably looked very different . . . Fate had been unkind to Jane Rule. With Elinor bedridden, likely to die at any moment, and Agnes seemingly in good physical shape, Jane had good reason to feel secure. But Agnes had stolen a march on her and died first. How long before Elinor, it was impossible to say, though Franks might be able to help there.

A clapped-out Mini with scarcely any lights, whining in second, charged the slope and forced him against the wall. 'Oaf!'

Anyway Jane was equal to the occasion. With Agnes in the freezer she put about the notion that the old lady was in the habit of wandering off, then she simply sat back, waiting for Elinor to die. If anybody called, Agnes was in bed asleep.

If he and Kersey hadn't blundered in when they did, looking for Hilda Clemo, a few days after Elinor's death Jane would have reported Agnes missing. There would have been a search, but nothing found. Agnes would have been added to the list of elderly missing persons, bound to turn up sometime — on a beach, in a ditch, or at the foot of a cliff.

Jane couldn't have kept the body in her freezer indefinitely; in any case she would have had no chance of getting leave to presume death, so with winter on the way, the visitors gone home and few people about, Agnes's body would have been dumped in some ditch — probably somewhere on the farm — and one day, come spring or early summer, Clifford, doing a spot of ditching, would — surprise, surprise! — come across the decaying remains of his Auntie Agnes, too far gone to retain any trace of her stay in the freezer.

It hung together but where did Hilda Clemo come in? Did she come in at all?

Wycliffe had reached the main street of the village where shops and cafés were still doing a lively trade. He was in search of Lily Armitage who had been Agnes Rule's regular Sunday visitor. He came upon a stocky figure wearing overalls and a peaked cap, seated on a window-sill, smoking his pipe.

'Could you tell me where Albert Place is?'

The man removed his pipe from his mouth, looked him up and down, and said: 'Who d'y want?'

'Lily Armitage.'

'Up that street, first turning on your right. Lily lives in the third house.'

Lily Armitage was seventy-eight; she lived with her unmarried daughter in one of a terrace of small cottages opposite a chapel. She was crippled with arthritis but mentally alert, even nimble. At one time she must have been big-boned and upright, now her frame was wasted and deformed though her facial features were still strong and her eyes were a rich brown. She had already heard the news along with everybody else.

'I've known Agnes all my life; we went to school together but when she went to Plymouth to keep house for Henry we lost touch. Of course we exchanged Christmas cards and such like but I didn't see much of her for nearly forty years. Then, when her brother died and she came to live with Jane at the farm, I took up to visit her — I used to go there most Sundays. She was all right then.'

'When was the last time you went to the farm?'

Her daughter had gone into the kitchen to make tea and the old lady called to her: 'How long is it since I stopped going to see Agnes?'

The answer came: 'The last time was in January, in the cold spell.'

'There you are then, it must be seven or eight months ago.' Lily was smoothing the red velvet arm of her chair with a crippled hand in which the veins stood out like cords. 'She'd gone queer, very queer. I know I moan enough about my arthritis but thank

95

God I've still got my wits! Sometimes Agnes wouldn't know me, once or twice she thought I was her mother . . . She had all sorts of silly notions.'

Wycliffe was seated opposite the old lady in an identical armchair, upholstered in red velvet. There was just space in the little parlour for the two chairs, a settee, and a chiffonier. An electric fire on the hearth made the room uncomfortably warm.

'I suppose Jane couldn't stand it any longer, but it was a terrible thing to do — terrible! And she must've known she'd be found out, surely?'

'Agnes Rule may well have died a natural death, Mrs Armitage. What was her attitude to her sister-in-law? How did they get on?'

'Before or after Agnes went queer?'

'Both.'

Lily shook her head. 'It's hard to say. Two women in the same house usually find it difficult, but as far as I could see they got on all right. Agnes kept herself to herself — I mean she had her own room and I suppose she was paying her way so there was no sort of friction over that . . . Of course Jane isn't the easiest woman to live with . . .'

'And after Agnes got queer in the head?'

'Ah, then she took against Jane. She used to say all sorts of things about her.'

'Such as?'

'Well, silly things — like Jane had ill-wished her, that she was trying to starve her, that she was stealing from her. She'd say: "When she's got everything she'll have me put away."'

'Did you believe any of that?'

Lily was emphatic. 'No!' But she added after a moment: 'Now, of course, you don't know what to think.'

Lily's daughter, a plump, comfortable woman of fifty (who must have taken after her father), brought in a tray with tea, gingerbread biscuits, and floral china on a lace-edged tray-cloth.

'I stopped mother going up there, Mr Wycliffe. It used to upset her too much. Help yourself to milk and sugar if you take it . . .'

'What other things did Agnes complain about?'

'She said Jane had changed her room around, that she'd interfered with the pictures — '

'And had she?'

'She'd spring-cleaned the room — not before it was needed, I can tell you! She might have put the furniture and pictures back a bit different.' Lily sighed. 'But Agnes was a long way from normal, Mr Wycliffe.'

Wycliffe held his cup and saucer in one hand and a Cornish gingerbread in the other. The daughter sat on the settee, blandly unobtrusive.

'Was Hilda Clemo ever mentioned in your conversations with Agnes?'

'Hilda! There's another sad thing. You never know what you're going to hear next.'

'Did Agnes talk about her?'

'Hilda used to come and see her, and Agnes was pleased about that because Hilda was a cut above her relatives, if you understand me. But she seemed to take to Agnes. After she went weak in the head Agnes would say: "Jane stopped young Hilda coming to see me." I heard that most every visit, and another time she said: "It'll be all right when Hilda comes; I shall tell her what's going on. She'll understand." '

'Just one more question, Mrs Armitage: do you know who Esther Clemo is? I mean, do you know who her parents were?'

The old lady looked at him in surprise. 'You don't know? Most anybody in the village could have told you about her mother, anyway. Her mother was a Tregenza from over Pentewan way.'

'And her father?'

'I doubt if anybody knew.' A hoarse chuckle. 'Esther came from what they call a one-parent family. They didn't have such things in my day.'

'Not a Clemo?'

A shrewd look. 'I've never heard anything of the sort.'

'I understand Esther worked for a time at Tregelles, then the Clemos adopted her. Why? A girl of sixteen?'

Lily pursed her lips. 'Now that *is* a question and a lot of people have asked it without getting any answer.'

It was almost ten o'clock when Wycliffe joined Kersey in The Seineis for a last drink before climbing the hill back to the hotel and bed.

PC Warren, not in uniform, but wearing jeans and an anorak and carrying a haversack which contained a flask of coffee, a few sandwiches, a torch, and his personal radio, was prepared for a lonely night. A patrol car dropped him just beyond the entrance to the lane leading to Tregelles, and he was left to make his way on foot across the fields to come up on the farmhouse without being seen.

'Have a good kip!' The patrol car drew away.

It was after nine and twilight had all but given way to the advancing night; an orange flush in the sky, way beyond the Dodman, marked the last phase of the contest. He trudged along the margins of three fields where dozy cattle, settled for the night, turned their heads to watch him. There was still light enough for the pine trees behind the Innes place to provide a landmark. He skirted the trees; there were lights in the house and he could hear music. Another field, and he could see in dim outline the block of buildings which formed a square around the farmyard at Tregelles. Here, he came upon the footpath leading to the farm from the Gorran side and, a minute or two later, he was at the gate into the yard itself.

It seemed as good a base as any. He could see the whole front of the house and most of the yard, with plenty of cover nearby if he needed it. There was a light in a downstair room and through the uncurtained window he could see Jane Rule, seated at a table. She was sewing or darning, her right hand rose and fell as she plied her needle. Clifford was not in his field of view.

At a little after ten the light went out and another came on upstairs. Five or ten minutes later the house was in darkness. Vague rustlings, occasional squeaks and thuds and muted squawks came from the rabbits and the hens as they stirred uneasily in sleep. Warren made a cautious reconnaissance round the back of the house. Upstairs a light showed at one window, but was extinguished while he watched. Presumably both the

Rules were in bed. Warren returned to base and drank some of his coffee.

By one o'clock his coffee had run out and, shortly after that, he ate the last of his sandwiches. The night was still and silent, there was no moon, only the stars, but to Warren, his eyes accommodating to the light, it was almost like day. He could hear the sea, a gentle rippling sound as wavelets spread over the beach a mile away. Now and then a motor car sped along the road; once, an aeroplane droned overhead, but that was all.

He made another circuit of the property but this time, as he returned to the yard, a dog in the house started barking. He froze against a dark wall, but nothing happened; the dog, after a few valedictory yelps, settled again. Warren crept back to his base and his granite seat.

He looked at his watch at a little before three and it was then that he noticed an abrupt change. It had turned chilly, he could no longer see the stars and mist seemed to condense out of the air around him. Although there was no wind the mist swirled and eddied; sometimes it seemed to lift, only to close in again almost at once. After what seemed an age he looked at his watch again: ten minutes to four. He got up to restore the circulation in his legs and it was then that he heard what sounded like a distant splash. Somewhere a dog barked, but not for long. Was the splash worth noting? Better put something in the log to show that he'd stayed awake. 'At 03.53 hours I heard what sounded like a splash . . .'

After that he must have dozed, for the next time he looked into the farmyard he was astonished to see a stocky figure, quite motionless, standing in the middle of the yard. It was a man; through the mist and the darkness he could make out very little detail but the man was carrying a gun under his arm — a shotgun, broken at the breech.

Automatically Warren glanced at his watch; it was four thirty-two and there seemed to be a glimmer of light in the eastern sky.

Warren was uncertain what exactly he should do but his mind was made up for him. Abruptly, the man closed the breech of his gun and advanced towards the house. As he moved forward Warren burst through the gate and caught him at the door of the house. 'I am a police officer on surveillance duty; I'm asking you to give an account of yourself.' He was scared and must have sounded breathless.

For the first time he saw the man's face clearly. It was James Clemo from the caravan site. Clemo looked at the young policeman, his expression utterly blank, and said nothing.

'What are you doing here at this time of night, and why are you carrying a gun?'

Clemo still said nothing. The dog in the house started a furious barking. 'Hand over the gun, please, sir.'

A light went on upstairs.

Clemo made no move but he allowed Warren to take the gun from him without resistance. Warren breathed thanks to whatever saints make policemen their special concern, opened the breech, and removed the cartridge. Jane Rule's voice came from the house, shouting to her son and telling the dog to shut up. The door opened and she stood there in her nightgown, joined almost at once by her son.

'What's going on now, for God's sake?'

Chapter Seven

Wednesday morning

Esther woke with a start. Had she been dreaming? She could not remember but she sat up in bed, tense. The house was still and no sound came from the caravan park but she could just hear the distant, rhythmic murmur of the sea. There was no moon but light from the window filled the room with shapes and shadows. It fell obliquely on the statue of the Virgin and she crossed herself. 'Holy Mary, Mother of God . . .'

For days she had been conscious of the approach of evil, now it seemed like a physical presence — in her room. She got out of bed, pulled on a dressing-gown over her nightdress, and worked her feet into her slippers. Still in the darkness she genuflected before the Virgin, then left the room. James's room was next to hers and his door was a little open. She pushed it wider and looked in. She could see the bed, bedclothes thrown back. James was not there. Her lips moved: 'Please, God, don't let him . . .'

She went downstairs and through to the back of the house, to the room next to the kitchen which had been the farm office. So far she had moved about the house silently and in darkness, now she switched on a light. The old clock above James's desk showed twenty minutes past three. The door of the wall cupboard was open and the chain lock which had secured James's shotgun hung loose. The gun had gone.

'Oh God, don't let him!'

She hesitated, then made up her mind. From a cupboard in the back hall she fetched a pair of old shoes which she kept for gardening, and a tweed coat, which she put on over her dressing-gown. There was an electric torch, always kept on a shelf by the back door, and she picked it up as she let herself out.

It was misty, a sea mist that played tricks. The caravans were all in darkness but the site was lit by a number of lamps which glowed through the mist. She ran for the first couple of hundred yards then, panting, slowed to a walking pace. She passed under the trees, out of range of the lamps, and switched on her torch, but the mist threw its light back at her so that she seemed to be walking towards a luminous wall. She found it best to shine the light at her feet where the path was clearly visible but she felt vulnerable — a target. She told herself that this was nonsense and pressed on.

She could hear the stream to her right and gradually vague shapes seemed to differentiate out of the darkness until she could distinguish outlines of trees and an interlacing network of branches against the sky. She stepped out with greater confidence.

For a while, preoccupied with her difficulties, she had almost forgotten her purpose; now its urgency possessed her. The path broadened into a track; she had reached the quarry pool and its surface gleamed very faintly through the mist. There were sounds, tiny sounds, crepitations; and occasional little cracks like the snapping of small twigs. She still could not see more than a foot or two in front of her and she was scared. A small splash in the water close by startled her. A water vole? Although she had lived all her life in the country she knew very little of its wildlife.

'Please, God . . .' She breathed inarticulate prayers.

Suddenly there were loud scraping sounds, followed by dull thuds, then a great splash. It came from the other side of the pool. Birds that had been roosting took to chattering flight.

She stood motionless, paralyzed by fear. 'Holy Mary Mother of God . . .'

But nothing happened, and after a little while, she resumed her way; the track began to rise and the trees closed in on either side as she left the pool behind. At the top of the slope there were no more trees, she was on level ground in open country and, despite the mist, she was able to see where she was going. She felt better. She reached the point where the path from the quarry edge joined the track; now she was skirting the edge of a field; in a short time she would reach the stile and the farmyard. If she didn't find James, what would she do? What *could* she do?

Ahead she could just make out the familiar outlines of the buildings. She was within a few feet of the gate and the stile when there was a commotion in the farmyard followed by a male voice, tense and boyish: 'I am a police officer . . . I'm asking you to give an account of yourself . . .' In surprise: '*Mr Clemo*! What are you doing here at this time of night?' A dog in the house began barking. 'Hand over the gun, please, sir . . .'

Esther was standing by the gate, clutching at the bars for fear she might collapse. She was trembling all over and it seemed that her heart must burst.

Then came Jane Rule's harsh voice calling her son, and a moment or two later: 'What's going on now, for God's sake?'

It was all right!

Her first impulse was to join the others in the farmyard, then she thought what James would say. In any case she couldn't face explanations. When she had sufficient control of her legs she made her way back along the track, and she was about to turn down the slope to the pool when she saw a figure in the mist only a few yards from her.

They had become mutually aware at the same instant and both stood stock still; then Esther, in sheer panic, took to her heels and ran. Once, she tripped and fell, banging her head on a root, but she picked herself up and ran again, blindly it seemed, until at last she emerged from the trees into the caravan park.

Already the sky was beginning to lighten but there was nobody about. She made what haste she could through the park down to the house, and let herself in by the back door. She stood inside, her back pressed against the door. She was panting, her chest felt unbearably constricted, and blood trickled down her temple and over her cheek.

Jeff Moyle was on his way to work at the caravan site. He lived not far from the Rules' farmhouse and regularly took the short cut over their fields and through the trees. Heavy rain the day before had drenched the undergrowth and, although the sun was gathering strength, the mist lingered.

Jeff was seventeen; he had been at school with Hilda Clemo but had left in the fifth form. Now he worked at her father's caravan site and Hilda was still a focus for his erotic fancies, but she had never given him a second look. According to some, others had made it, but that was probably just talk. The Ralph Martin thing had come as a surprise; everybody had taken it for granted that Ralph didn't know what he had it for. Now he was being questioned about Hilda's disappearance; and one or two of Jeff's former mates, still at school, had been tackled by the police. Jeff wondered if his turn would come.

He reached the quarry. Oddly, there was no mist over the water and there were gaps in the green weed which usually covered the surface in summer. On Monday a police frogman had searched the pool for Hilda's body and Jeff shuddered at the thought. A year or two ago he and another boy had gone swimming in the quarry pool for a dare. The water was bitterly cold and, as he emerged, breathless and spluttering, from his first plunge, his face had come into contact with something large and smooth, and hideously clammy, floating just below the surface. For a long moment it had seemed that he could not get away from this nameless thing, and he had panicked, striking out wildly for the shore.

It had turned out to be only a dead dog, hairless from long immersion; but the experience lived on in his dreams.

They must think Hilda was dead.

Was it possible that one of the boys he knew, one of his mates . . .?

He felt scared and quickened his pace. Only self-respect stopped him breaking into a run. But he averted his eyes from the pool. Even so a pale patch, seen out of the corner of his eye, insisted on attention. There, twenty or so yards away, floating almost on the surface, was the naked body of a girl. He stopped and gazed, hypnotized. What he saw could have been beautiful; at that distance the body appeared unharmed, only very white and quite still; yet he was filled with a sense of horror such as he had never known. This was Hilda, the girl of his fantasies, but Hilda had become a thing, like the dog.

He could not have said how long the spell held him but at last he was able to turn away; then he took to his heels and ran.

He arrived at Reception just as Alice, deathly pale, was opening the office to deal with early departures.

The news of James Clemo's arrest reached Wycliffe at seven-thirty, while he was shaving, a time judged by the duty officer to strike a nice balance between unnecessary intrusion and unjustifiable delay. In the event, Kersey had taken the call.

'Our man picked him up in the farmyard at half-past four this morning, with a shotgun under his arm and a cartridge up the spout.'

'Was he violent?'

'Apparently not, but he says he intended to force the Rules to admit what they had done to his daughter.'

Wycliffe was puzzled. Why was Clemo so convinced that the Rules were involved? Was he the sort to go after somebody with a gun on a vague suspicion? He had a good deal to learn about the Clemos and the Rules.

Now, it was eight-fifteen and they were in the hotel dining-room, at a table by the window, poised over the harbour. Sky and sea were blue; there were powder-puff clouds, and gulls soared and swooped over a fishing boat unloading its catch. The little houses across the harbour were stacked in short terraces, one above the other, and the scene had all the ingredients of his childhood vision of 'the seaside'.

Wycliffe was removing the fat from his bacon and laying it on the side of his plate.

Kersey eyed the operation with interest. 'You're leaving the best part. My granny used to say: "Eat up the fat, boy, it's good for you." She lived to be ninety-four.'

Kersey was in a limbo of indecision as far as food was concerned, trapped between the disturbing precepts of his wife, supported by the health freaks, and the consoling old-wives' tales which he dredged up from the past.

105

'Did she smoke?'

'What?'

'Your granny — did she smoke?'

'Good God, no!'

'There you are then.'

His thoughts returning to the case, Wycliffe went on: 'We must talk to Esther. If anybody knows what's going on with Clemo, she does. Incidentally, I was told last night that she worked at the Rules' as a girl of fifteen, before she was taken in by the Clemos.'

'Does that mean anything to us?'

'I've no idea.'

It was a popular time for breakfast, especially among families with children, and there was too much chatter for them to be overheard, but they were aware of being pointed out by the knowledgeable. So, when the manager, with exaggerated discretion, made his way to their table and bent over Wycliffe with a whispered message, all eyes were upon them.

'I'm sorry to disturb you, Chief Superintendent, but there is a telephone call for you . . . You will be quite private in my office . . .'

By nine o'clock Wycliffe was at the quarry with Kersey and Sergeant Fox, the scenes-of-crime officer. Fox was blighted by a non-existent chin, and a nose like Mr Punch. He was good at his job, but his pedantic manner and his self-assurance irritated Wycliffe.

Uniformed men from subdivision stood around, waiting to be useful. One man was paddling over the dark water in an inflatable, towards the body, while Dr Hosking, the police surgeon, stood at the margin, shouting instructions. Hosking was a little red-headed man with freckles and a fiery temper.

'No need to touch her! Just nuzzle the body along in this direction until we can reach it . . .' Then, to the men near him: 'Spread that plastic sheet on the grass, damn you!'

The sun was shining through the trees but the water absorbed much of the light so that the body of the girl seemed strikingly lit by contrast.

One of the constables muttered: 'Poor little bastard!'

The photographer's camera clicked and whirred as the body was eased out of the water to sag limply on the plastic sheeting.

Hilda Clemo. Wycliffe gazed down at all that remained of her; water weeds clung to her pale flesh and tangled with her hair. She had been murdered; he had no need of medical opinion to tell him that. Not that there was any compelling evidence of violence, but how else could she have ended up naked in the quarry pool?

The doctor was speaking to him. 'I thought you had a frogman here on Monday.'

The man who had crewed the inflatable said: 'It was me, sir. She wasn't here then.'

Kersey snapped: 'You'd better be right, lad!'

Hosking was crouching over the body. 'He probably is. She hasn't been in the water long. Franks might give you a better idea but I'd say less than twelve hours.'

Men had been stationed at all the approaches to the quarry; others were questioning people living nearby — the Rules, the Inneses, and the Moyles; also campers and caravanners on the site who had spent the night anywhere near the entrance to the wood. Did they see or hear anything suspicious or unusual? Were they themselves out and about at any time after dark? James Clemo was known to have made his way from his house to the farm during the night, had anyone seen him?

Hosking was carrying on with his job: 'As you see, there are multiple injuries, including limb fractures; most of those injuries were, in my opinion, incurred *post mortem*.'

'Most of them?'

'I'm not a magician, not even a pathologist. You'll have to ask Franks if you want detail.' He looked up at the virtual cliff which was the wall of the quarry. For the most part it was stepped, with ash and sycamore saplings growing on the ledges, but there was one place where the slope was steeper and more or less uniform, broken only by occasional jagged spurs of rock. Hosking pointed: 'My guess is that she was tumbled off there.'

It was the only place where there was a gap in the screen of bushes and sapling trees, around the quarry edge.

'Look at these.' Hosking pointed to marks on the girl's neck on either side of the windpipe, just below the larynx.

Wycliffe said: 'You are not suggesting that she might have been strangled?'

'Hardly, but the marks are interesting.' He had turned his attention to superficial injuries to the face and limbs — abrasions and lacerations — and to patches of slight discoloration on the lower abdomen. Then he parted the fair hair near the crown of the head, exposing a crescent-shaped depression in the skull with a swollen margin. Despite the immersion there were still traces of congealed blood at the roots of the hair.

The photographer was following the doctor's examination with his camera.

Hilda Clemo had become the property of experts.

Wycliffe said: 'What do you make of the head wound?'

'It's not up to me, but I can't find anything else that might have killed her. Anyhow, the sooner you get her to the mortuary and Franks takes over, the better. Isn't the van here yet?'

As he spoke two men arrived with a stretcher and a plastic shell. 'It's easier to carry her to the van than to bring the van up here.'

So, wrapped in a plastic envelope on a makeshift bier, Hilda Clemo was carried away. A sergeant accompanied the body to maintain continuity of evidence.

Hardly known outside her village, this schoolgirl was about to enter the professional ken of dozens, scores, and eventually hundreds of total strangers. Their only interest would be to identify and convict the person responsible for her death and, that done, she would be forgotten. The spotlight would be on her killer and the climax would come in a courtroom melodrama with the killer as the star.

Sometimes it seemed to Wycliffe that it was a very odd machine in which he was a small cog. But how could it be otherwise?

The routine of a murder investigation was under way: a report would go to the coroner; the coroner would issue a warrant for the autopsy in the name of Dr Franks, the pathologist; a policeman, functioning as coroner's officer, would maintain liaison between him and the police. Meanwhile the remains of Hilda Clemo were being put to rest in a refrigerated drawer awaiting the gross indignities that would be inflicted on her in the interests of justice. A procedure which would do neither her nor her family any good at all.

Wycliffe and Kersey walked up the valley, away from the others. Kersey kicked a small branch into the stream, still swollen and turbulent after the rain, and watched it being swirled away.

'So the girl is dead. And it certainly looks like murder. I suppose the Rules are our obvious suspects.'

'But the body must have been pushed into the quarry pool last night. PC Warren thought he heard a splash at a few minutes before four. Are you suggesting that Clifford got out of the house and back in again under Warren's nose? Remember he was with his mother when Warren created a stir in disarming Clemo.'

'Clemo got into the yard without being seen, didn't he? These young coppers are a dozy lot.'

'And the motive for killing the girl in the first place?'

Kersey shrugged. 'Rape. The half-wit attacked and raped her. He seems gentle enough but I suppose he has sexual urges like the rest of us — and no outlet. Of course the cover-up would be Mother's doing. It's significant that the girl's body should turn up this morning. Jane must have thought last night would be their last chance to dispose of it; with Agnes out of the bag, so to speak, she knew that she was in trouble; she must have realized that she was very lucky to have that last chance.'

Wycliffe was sceptical. 'Where was the body when we went over the house yesterday? Remember Rowse claims to have done a thorough job with the outhouses and in the neighbouring fields.'

'He didn't find Agnes, did he?' Kersey said, with a ferocious grin. 'Come to think of it — if the girl had found out about the old lady it could have been a motive for both of them.'

Wycliffe shook his head. After a moment or two he said: 'At

least when Franks does his autopsy he should be able to type the embryo against possible candidates for its paternity.'

Wycliffe and Kersey stood close to the spot from where it seemed that Hilda Clemo's nude body had been pushed over the edge, to roll down the slope in hazard of the rocky spurs, and splash into the dark pool below. They were all but surrounded by gorse in brilliant flower and the bees, like the villagers, were busy on the last lap of treadmill before autumn really set in.

A faded notice on a broken post read 'Danger!' And danger there was, for the ground ended abruptly at the quarry edge. Fox pointed to the evidence, which was plain enough. The heavy rain of the previous day had left the immediate approach to the quarry edge soft and muddy. A square groove in the mud, about an inch and a quarter wide, was clearly defined for a distance of nine or ten feet, until it reached the footpath where the ground was compact and stony.

'That groove was made by the iron rim of an old-style wheelbarrow, sir.'

In addition to the wheel mark there were confused impressions; some of them might have been partially obliterated footprints, others could have been made by the body of the girl as it was dragged to the edge. But, superimposed on all this, there were clear and unmistakable footprints.

'Clifford Rule's wellies,' Kersey said.

The patterns in the mud had been photographed; now Fox and his assistant were making plaster casts. Uniformed men were searching the grass and scrub, working away from the quarry edge and along the footpath.

From where he stood, now that he knew the lay-out of the countryside, Wycliffe could identify the farm buildings at Tregelles, the Innes place with its attendant pine trees, and the cottage and ramshackle sheds belonging to the Moyles. He could see the tower of Gorran church away to the west and, to the south, the gleaming horizon of the sea. Somehow it was not a setting for tragedy and yet, in the last few hours, someone had wheeled the naked body of a murdered girl to the quarry and tipped it over the edge like a sack of rubbish.

They walked back along the path for a couple of hundred yards to where it joined the broad track coming up from the stream and the quarry pool.

'You see, sir,' Fox said, 'anyone coming from, say the farm, wheeling the barrow, had a choice. He could take the footpath to the edge of the quarry and tip the body over, or he could go down the track into the valley and ditch it in the pool with less commotion. Our chap chose the earlier option.'

Wycliffe cut him short. 'Where does this one go?' Yet another path which seemed to lead away from the quarry inland, towards the Gorran road.

Fox reluctantly admitted to something less than certainty. 'I'm not sure, sir. The place is like a maze, but from the map I think it goes round the back of the quarry and down to the caravan park that way.'

Wycliffe was reflective. 'We are assuming that, dead or alive, the girl spent three nights and days hidden within a few hundred yards from where we are standing; then, last night, she was brought here already dead, in Fox's hypothetical wheelbarrow.'

Fox nodded. 'It seems obvious, doesn't it, sir?'

Kersey said: 'Well, there they are: the Rules, the Inneses, and the Moyles, the only people within reasonable range. But I wouldn't fancy wheeling a barrow with a girl's body in it along these tracks in the middle of the night.'

Fox said: 'It's very nearly level ground.'

They were interrupted by a shout from one of the uniformed men who had been poking about among nettles and brambles beside the footpath. Wycliffe and Kersey went over with Fox. The constable was holding a little wooden carving of a cow. The form of the creature had been roughed out and detailed carving had begun with the head.

Kersey took the carving from the constable. 'It would be nice to know when he lost it.'

Wycliffe was morose. 'Then you'd better ask him. Get hold of a DC and, starting with the Rules — Anyway, you don't need me

111

to tell you what to do. Get what assistance you need; Lucy Lane is at the house but she should be available shortly.'

He sighed, taking another look around him. 'I'm going back to the van. It's time I put the chief in the picture and I expect to hear from Franks. Shaw is trying to set up an Incident Room on North Quay and I want to see what's happening about that . . .' For a few minutes they discussed organization.

When Wycliffe left he decided to follow the path which Fox thought must lead back to the caravan park by a different route, circling and avoiding the quarry.

It was easy walking, a gentle downward slope between bramble bushes where blackberries were ripening. He walked slowly, feeling guilty because the sun was shining, warm on his skin, and because Hilda Clemo was dead.

Hilda Clemo was dead. But why? Because she was pregnant? What other reason could there be? Unless it was a case of rape, but rapists do not, as a rule, quieten their victims by a blow on the back of the head . . .

In a surprisingly short space of time the scrub gave way to open grassland and a neat notice: 'Tregwythen Leisure Park. Nine-hole Golf Course. Walkers please keep to the path.' A well-made track followed the undulations of the course leading to a long, low building, close to the margins of the wood, and to the first of the caravans. Nearer at hand there were tennis courts and a swimming-pool with a diving-board.

So the quarry edge was approachable from the caravan park by a route which, though longer, was certainly less arduous. In a very few minutes Wycliffe reached the building. It seemed to be an implements store and shop and on the shop door there was a notice: 'Open 11 a.m. until Dusk'. Another hundred yards and he had joined the main road through the park.

Already uniformed men were making the rounds of caravans and tents with clipboards. The atmosphere was subdued; the discovery of the girl's body had cast a pall over the place; this, on top of the gruesome finding of an old woman in a freezer at the farm. Though the sun was shining and it was pleasantly warm there were no children playing out of doors and he could hear no radios. But he was conscious of being watched. He was a link with those sombre events which had taken place only a short distance away, and many of the caravanners had been on the site long enough to have known the girl whose body had been retrieved from the flooded quarry . . .

Wycliffe drove slowly back to the harbour. Even after thirty-odd years in the force he was still profoundly shocked and saddened by murder. He navigated through the square and through one of the narrow alleys which led to the harbour. On the quay he had to squeeze past a fish lorry, his nearside wheels creeping along the quay edge. He saw in his mind's eye a headline in the local paper: 'Police Chief in Harbour Tragedy', and breathed a sigh of relief when he was through.

By bush telegraph or ESP the press had got to hear of the discovery of the girl's body and two reporters were picketing the Incident Van.

'All I can tell you is that the young woman's death is believed to have been due to foul play so this is a murder investigation.'

'A sex crime?'

'I don't know — and that is the truth.'

'Was the body naked?'

'Yes.'

'Badly mutilated?'

'No.'

'The girl has been missing for four days, when did she actually die?'

'I hope the pathologist will tell me that.'

'Was she drowned?'

'I think not but I am not a pathologist.'

'Is it true that a police frogman searched the quarry pool on Monday, and found nothing?'

'Yes.'

'Why didn't he find the body then?'

'Probably because it wasn't there.'

'Yesterday the police found a woman's body in a freezer at Tregelles Farm. Is there a connection?'

'I've no idea. I don't know yet how the woman died or when.'

'Died, or was murdered?'

'The post-mortem and the coroner will decide that.'

'Jane Rule and her son are not in custody?'

'No, they are not.'

'Is it true that the son is a half-wit?'

'I'm not a psychologist. And that's all I've got for you at the moment, I'll talk to you again when there's more. Anyway, there's plenty for your imaginations to work on as it is.'

They let him go, in good humour. In the van DC Dixon gave him a little sheaf of memo slips with telephone messages. One was from Franks, the pathologist. It read: 'On my way; be with you before noon.' Dramatic as ever.

Another message was from the Chief Constable asking him to telephone, which he did.

Bertram Oldfield was Wycliffe's chief, also a friend, but the two roles were never allowed to tangle.

'I want you to look in this evening, Charles. Sampson has raised one or two legal quibbles about our submission to the DPP in the Archer–Burrows case. We can do without any cock-ups in that direction so I've arranged for a vetting session here at about half-six.

'Now, just put me in the picture about your case, Charles.'

Wycliffe did so, and answered almost the same questions as the reporters had asked.

'It's an end-of-season gift to the media, Charles, so watch your step. Get your Incident Room organized, have the TV cameras in. Let 'em see the line-up of VDU screens, grim-faced officers pecking away at keyboards, telephones ringing . . . I know how you hate it, so do I, but it helps to convince the public that we're on their side. Look at TV's *Crimewatch* — it even catches villains.'

Wycliffe was old-fashioned; he liked to rely on a few people following clearly defined lines of enquiry rather than on a small army feeding a computer and hoping to press the right keys for the jackpot. He conceded that the computer method might be good for wide-open cases, say the rape and murder of a girl

114

hitcher off a motorway, but the investigation of crime in a small community must be more personal, so much depends on individual contacts and individual assessments.

An expensive throbbing sound announced the arrival of Dr Franks in his Porsche. Although they had worked together for years Wycliffe felt vaguely uncomfortable at each fresh encounter. The two men could hardly have been more different: Franks had an acceptance philosophy; he was at home in the world, and rather liked it, while Wycliffe had an uneasy feeling that he was picking his way, blindfold, across a tight-rope.

'The Chief in?' — Franks in the outside cubicle.

DC Dixon came to announce him with Franks on his heels.

'Charles! I was about to telephone about your frozen old woman when they told me that you had another body for me so I thought I'd come down. A girl, this time, isn't it?'

Franks was a roly-poly man, immaculately turned out, and smelling of aftershave.

'I wanted a word. First about your old lady: she died of a massive cerebral haemorrhage probably triggered by a nasty fit of coughing — there was a good deal of mucus in the air passages. I'd guess that she was swallowing something which went the wrong way; she managed to clear it, but too late.'

'No sign of violence?'

'None; and no indications of poison. She died a natural death.'

'When?'

'What do you mean, when?'

'Time of death.'

Franks looked at him wide-eyed. 'You must be joking! If you asked me for a date I couldn't give it to you, let alone a time. I can say that she was put in the freezer within a very few hours of death.'

'Any signs of internal putrefaction?'

'You don't imagine that with a thing the size of a human body, freezing could be instantaneous?'

'No, I don't, but forensic technicians removed her from the freezer so presumably you were given enough data to balance the rate of putrefaction against the rate of penetration and give me some sort of estimate of how long she was in there.'

Franks grinned. 'You've learned a lot from me in the last fifteen years, Charles. At a guess — and it's no more — I'd say she'd been in the box for two to three weeks.'

'Certainly more than a week?'

'Definitely.'

'And you'll say that in court if necessary?'

'With pleasure.'

'Good! That's all I need. Now about the girl — how long before I get a preliminary report?'

'Seeing she isn't frozen solid, say late this afternoon.'

'Thanks. So, until then . . .'

'Don't be in such a damned hurry, Charles! I came here mainly to tell you that I knew Agnes Rule when she was a young woman. Until this morning, dictating my report, I hadn't really taken any notice of the subject's name. Then I made one or two enquiries to make sure I had the right one.'

'How did you come to know her?'

'When I was a boy my father had a book shop next door to Henry Rule's antiques shop.'

'In Plymouth?'

'Of course, in Queen Mary Street.'

It was the first time Wycliffe had heard Franks mention his family and it came as a mild surprise to realize that he must have had one.

'Henry was a bachelor, living over his shop with his sister, Agnes, to housekeep for him. My people used to invite them out for Sunday lunch — that sort of thing. Later, when Henry decided to show off some of his stock in a domestic setting, he and Agnes moved into a biggish house, Devonport way.'

'I gather he made money.'

'Made it and spent it or gambled it away on the gee-gees. During the war he bought up the salvaged contents of blitzed properties in a big way and, after the war, when people were trying to get started again with everything in short supply, he made a bomb unloading the stuff. It was that and other things that turned father against him.'

'What other things?'

'His business methods generally upset father who was very strait-laced. Henry employed "knockers" — characters who toured the countryside persuading impoverished old ladies to part with their valuables at more or less junk prices. It was a lucrative business in those days, the new poor weren't very well versed in the ways of the world. Sometimes it was outright theft and, on at least two occasions, Henry was within a cat's whisker of being done for receiving.'

Franks stood up. 'Well, there it is for what it's worth.'

'Thanks, it could be useful.'

Franks grinned. 'One way and another I spoon-feed you, Charles, and what do you do for me? Now I'm going to take you out to lunch.'

Wycliffe held his peace.

Lucy Lane had arrived at the Clemos shortly after the discovery of Hilda Clemo's body and while Clemo was still detained at St Austell following his arrest in the early hours. Alice, close to hysteria at first, had come to terms with the situation and was finding some relief in the essential routine of the site office. Esther, more than ever resembling a walking corpse, went about her household tasks and looked after the little boy. She had a fresh bruise on her forehead and a bandage on one hand. Lucy had not seen Bertie who was out on the site.

At eleven o'clock Clemo arrived home, released on police bail. He had insisted on being taken first to the mortuary where he had identified his daughter's body.

Lucy and WPC Milly Rees from subdivision were making a detailed search of Hilda's room. Every cupboard, every shelf and every drawer was emptied, its contents examined and put back. At one point Clemo came and stood in the doorway; for a minute or two he watched them with a bewildered expression then, without a word, he went away again.

Milly Rees said: 'Funny girl she must've been.'

'Why funny?'

Milly Rees was a plump, bosomy girl, tailor-made for the modern world, and a little suspicious of those who were not.

'Odd, I mean. It's all so damn dull. A place for everything and all that. Seventeen, she was! If you don't have a good time then, when do you? And clothes — I mean, she didn't have any to speak of. If I open one of my cupboards I got to stand back quick. And I've got part of mother's wardrobe too. I suppose there must be all kinds but it's hard to see where she got her kicks . . . Look at her cassettes — I mean . . . And her books . . . And no make-up that I've seen.'

'She was a very clever girl.'

'God! She'd need to be. Personally I'd rather be dumb and happy.'

Each drawer was turned upside down and inspected before being put back and it was Lucy who scored there.

'Look at this.'

An A4 envelope was pinned to the underside of the bottom drawer of the desk.

Lucy removed the envelope. It was unsealed and she drew out a pencil sketch and a letter on National Gallery headed paper. The sketch was more like a labelled diagram competently done, and showed a road through a village with houses, a couple of horses and carts, a grassy verge, trees and figures. In the bottom left-hand corner there was a copy of a signature with a date: 'C Pissarro 1876'. Labelled arrows indicated colours, and at the top of the sketch, dimensions were given: '18″ x 21‴'. With the statement: 'Painted in oils'.

The letter was dated the previous January and read:

'Dear Miss Clemo,

'I regret that we are unable to offer an opinion about a picture based on the evidence of a sketch or, indeed, on any evidence other than the picture itself. If you are able to bring the picture to London I suggest that you bring it here, or take it to one of the major salerooms where you would get expert advice as to its provenance and probable value. There are also competent people among the fine art auctioneers nearer your home who would help you.

'Your sketch is reminiscent of a number of pictures painted

by Pissarro, in the late sixties and in the seventies of the last century, in and around the village of Pontoise. However, I am afraid that means nothing in terms of the genuineness or otherwise of your picture.

'Sincerely, Squiggle, Assistant Curator.'

Milly said: 'What's that all about?'

'I don't know, but I fancy we're going to have to find out.'

It was in the bottom drawer of a small chest, under a collection of winter woollies, that Milly found another envelope, this one contained a dozen or so photographs, mostly of Hilda herself as a little girl, toddler to teenager — just. Milly flicked through them without interest then let out a whistle. 'What about this, then? Full frontal and all.' She held out an enprint of a nude man, facing the camera.

Lucy took it. 'That's Bertie, her brother-in-law.'

'Well, he looks all right to me. Perhaps after all she'd realized there was life before death. But I wonder what big sister would think about it?'

'There's your barrow, sir.' DC Dixon to Kersey.

In Tregelles farmyard, in one of the open sheds, between the old tractor and Jane Rule's Morris Minor, there was a rusty barrow with an iron wheel, spattered in hen droppings.

Kersey said: 'You think so? Try pushing it, lad; it'll make a racket like a tone-deaf drunk playing the "Soldier's Lament" on the bagpipes . . . Go on!'

Dixon wheeled the barrow out of the shed into the yard to a protesting chorus of squeaks and squeals from bearings which had forgotten there was such a thing as grease.

Kersey said: 'I'll bet they heard that in the village. The thing weighs half a ton, anyway.'

'What you want it for?'

Clifford had come out of the house to watch, mildly inquisitive. Kersey looked down at his wellies. 'What were you doing at the quarry this morning?'

'I heard some shouting and went over to see what it was about. They was policemen and I think they found Hilda.'

'You didn't stay to find out?'

'I saw two of 'em coming up to where I was so I come back here and told Mother.'

'Did you lose this?' Kersey held out the little cow-carving found near the edge of the quarry.

Clifford looked at it with interest. 'Not then.'

'When?'

He shook his head. 'I dunno.'

Jane Rule came out of the house and crossed the yard. 'What is it now?' She was wearied to the verge of collapse and her face was grey.

'We'd better go inside,' Kersey said.

Once more the Rules sat at their kitchen table faced with two policemen and once more Clifford brought out his clasp knife, but sheepishly, with his eye on his mother.

Kersey said: 'We believe that you have been selling items of furniture belonging to your sister-in-law, Miss Agnes Rule. I have to caution you. You do not have to say anything but what you do say may be taken down and used in evidence.'

Kersey thought: 'What do I care if she flogged the old woman's furniture? This is a bloody charade. Either her precious son raped and killed the girl or he didn't; that's what all this is about.'

Jane Rule said: 'There's no point in denying it; I've no reason to. After Agnes went queer she wouldn't give me any money except her old age pension, which I collected anyway. She had her room, her food, and she was waited on hand and foot — everything I had to do for her. And then she accused me of stealing from her. What do you expect? In any old people's home it would have cost somebody four or five times her pension for what she got.'

'So what did you sell?'

Jane shrugged her thin shoulders. 'A couple of things — a bureau and a table.'

'You sold them through Bertie Harvey?'

'He said he could get a good price.'

'What did he give you?'

'For the bureau I got two hundred, and for the table, one-fifty. That and her pension was all I had to keep her for a year, and the things would've been mine anyway when she died.'

'Only if she'd outlived her sister. Why didn't you go to her lawyer about money?'

'I hate lawyers.'

It was strange. The woman was guilty of concealing a death in a barbarous fashion and with intent to defraud; she was guilty too of disposing of property without the consent of the owner. And yet, Kersey felt sure, all she had done seemed to her logical and reasonable. What struck him as odder still, was that he was half inclined to agree with her.

Chapter Eight

Wednesday afternoon

A crab salad and a bottle of Barsac was the limit set by Wycliffe on the pathologist's hospitality. With it came unsolicited advice: 'You can't change the world, Charles, so why not go with the current? It's too late for poking fingers into dykes; too late to start building a bloody ark. We're all being swept along by the flood, God knows where, but there are still good bits, so make the most of 'em.'

Afterwards Wycliffe felt mellowed, but that was the Barsac. 'Don't forget to phone me as soon as you have anything on the girl. She was pregnant and I'm anxious for you to type the embryo and match it against possible fathers.'

'Rely on me, Charles; I should have something for you by this evening.'

'Then ring me at home.'

The Porsche took off with a screech of tyres, the Franks signature tune.

Wycliffe felt a little like the White Rabbit and wondered why he always let Franks get away with it.

They were now installed in an empty shop premises on the North Quay. DS Shaw, with the help of central stores and a brace of technicians, had established a home from home for displaced coppers. The fascia board over the shop was faded but the sign was still legible: 'Charlie's Whatnot: Knick-knacks and By-gones'. Some clown, in or out of the Force, would make something of that. Anyway it was a definite improvement on the van. On the ground floor there were tables, word processors, and

122

telephones, with accommodation for seven or eight officers. Up the rickety stairs, a room, with its own computer link, had been set aside for the senior officer, and another for interviews. Luxury! There was even a tiny kitchen where Potter, the squad's fat man, was already brewing tea.

The duty officer said: 'There's a Mr Delbos of Exeter trying to contact you, sir. He's left a number and wants you to ring back.'

Delbos . . . The name was familiar but, for a moment, he couldn't place it, then he remembered: Lovell and Delbos, Bertie Harvey's former employers.

'Get him for me, please.'

A suave gentleman, and elderly to judge from his voice. Wycliffe imagined him lean, tanned and military, with a well-trimmed white moustache.

'One of your officers was here this morning enquiring about a former employee of ours; I said that I would telephone you.'

Wycliffe made appropriate noises, and: 'It would be helpful to know whether he left you of his own accord or was dismissed.'

Hesitation. 'He was not dismissed; let us say that he was encouraged to leave.'

'May I ask why?'

'Because he failed to live up to the professional standard of conduct we expect of our employees.'

'In what way?'

Some humming and hawing, then: 'We offer a free valuation service to the public. People can bring things to be valued without obligation. Harvey, in several instances, entered into private arrangements with prospective clients, bypassing the firm.'

'He bought the things himself?'

Hesitation. 'No, he was acting on behalf of certain unscrupulous dealers who use such methods — that is to say, they bribe employees of other firms to act as scouts.'

'Did he specialize in any particular branch of the fine arts trade?'

'We are a smallish firm, Mr Wycliffe, but Harvey was mainly concerned with porcelain and pictures.'

Wycliffe found Kersey and Lucy Lane in the upper room. Kersey was depressed, and he looked tired. By afternoon each day he had a growth of dark bristles around his chin which in contrast with his sallow skin made him seem unnaturally pale.

'I've spent the morning trotting about up there: the Rules, the Moyles, the Inneses — isn't she the oddest little thing? And, of course, I've talked to our friend, Bertie Harvey.'

'And?'

'That's just it. Nix! You feel we're missing out all along the line. Fox isn't getting anywhere either. I've had another look at that wheel track of his. I don't think it's a wheel track at all. I made an exactly similar rut with a piece of wood.'

'A plant?'

'I'm sure of it — like the little carving. Somebody's being naughty; too damn clever — like most amateurs.'

'The fact remains that the girl's body was moved, one way or another, to the quarry pool last night. The snag is nobody saw anything, or heard anything except the splash, least of all our dozy wooden-top who must have had a grandstand seat for most that went on.'

Wycliffe said: 'With a plank and a couple of pram wheels you can move almost anything, and without waking the neighbourhood.'

Lucy Lane looked up from sorting reports. 'What about Mrs Innes's wheelchair?'

'I suppose that's possibe,' Wycliffe agreed. 'But we may have things the wrong way round. We're assuming the girl's body was kept in the neighbourhood of the farm; what if it was hidden somewhere on the caravan site?'

Kersey grimaced. 'Bertie?'

'Where was he last night?'

'Tucked up in bed by midnight, according to him. We could check with his wife if that's any use.'

'He doesn't sleep with his wife.'

'Ah! You have inside knowledge, sir. But who in their right mind would hump the body all round the pool, up the slope, and along the top path just to push it over the edge with a splash?'

'He wouldn't have to; there's a perfectly good way to the quarry through the golf course. Anyway, what else did you get?'

Kersey reported and Wycliffe listened.

'So Jane Rule admits selling and Bertie Harvey admits handling the sale of a table and bureau?'

'Yes, and there's probably more. No doubt she's technically guilty of dishonest handling or some bloody thing, but it doesn't help us. And Harvey says how was he to know the stuff wasn't Jane's?'

'Get someone to check exactly what the items were, where he sold them, and the prices he got.'

'I've laid that on, sir, but what good will it do us?'

'It's ammunition. What did you make of the Inneses?'

Kersey frowned. 'An odd couple! The mind, as they say, boggles. I couldn't make much of them; people like that are out of my league.' A sly glance at Lucy Lane. 'You need somebody with a bit more of the culture.'

Kersey's banter, never entirely free of malice, rarely missed a chance to knock Lucy's academic background. 'I sometimes think we should have a special squad to deal with witnesses who have more than five 0–levels.'

Wycliffe was used to it. 'It's now GCSEs or something. Anyway, the Inneses heard and saw nothing last night?'

'So they said.'

'Now, Lucy.'

Lucy Lane provided a rapid word picture of the situation at the Clemos. 'To add to the mix, Esther has a nasty cut and bruise on her forehead and she's injured her right hand. She says she fell down in the backyard.'

Lucy made a considerable impression with Hilda's pencil sketch and her letter from the gallery; also with the photograph of a nude Bertie.

'You've had them checked for prints, and photocopied?'

'Yes. There are several sets of prints on the sketch and the letter; only two on the photograph. The prints are being checked out.'

Kersey said: 'What sort of girl would keep a photo of a bloke like that?'

'The other way round would be all right, I suppose?' Lucy Lane, acid.

'More normal, anyhow.'

Wycliffe was impatient. 'Let's forget the battle of the sexes and concentrate on the facts. If there was a sexual relationship between Harvey and the girl — '

'There doesn't seem to be much "if" about it, sir, it seems obvious.'

'Perhaps. Anyway, another interview with Bertie; this time we must be in a position to lean on him a bit. Now the sketch and the letter from the National Gallery . . . Lucy?'

Lucy Lane rarely spoke without reflection, measured by the knitted brow. She turned the pages of her notebook which was unnecessary to her recall. 'Hilda must have had access to a painting, apparently by Pissarro, and wanted to know if it was genuine. She obviously didn't know much about pictures but probably realized that a Pissarro must be worth a lot of money.'

Kersey said: 'How much?'

'From what I've been able to find out, even a smallish oil like the one she sketched — eighteen by twenty-one inches — if well authenticated, would probably fetch two hundred thousand, perhaps more.'

Kersey whistled. 'God! That's money even in these days. Murder is being done for a hell of a lot less. If she was mixed up with some swindle on that scale . . .'

Wycliffe said: 'Hilda was a regular visitor at the farm until Agnes went queer, so it's possible she saw the picture there — the date of the letter fits. But, if so, where is it now?'

Kersey grinned. 'The States? Japan? South Korea? Taiwan?'

'You could be right at that. Now, as to what we do. I want you to find out from Penrose, the lawyer, whether he has an inventory of Henry Rule's stuff stored at the farm. If he has, have it checked by a qualified valuer. Don't mention this hypothetical picture or we shall have the press after us. If there's no inventory, then get one made. It probably won't help but it will show we mean business. If Penrose or the Rules make any difficulty, we want to know how much of Henry Rule's stuff did Jane sell. Has she purged her soul?'

'And then?'

'We'll see. Before we show our hand I want to have all the evidence we can get. With luck, by tomorrow, we should be in a position to tackle Bertie and bring Innes into play. After all, he's supposed to be the art expert.'

Kersey was standing by the window which, because the shop was built in the angle of the sea-wall, gave a clear view along the quay to the wharf. A red-head stood out, her small, thin, angular figure, dressed by Oxfam, aggressively purposeful in contrast with the ambling trippers.

'Ella's coming.'

Ella Bunt, a free-lance crime reporter who rated by-lines over a majority of inside crime stories. For years (and Ella was still in the thirties) Wycliffe had suffered her surprisingly benevolent patronage. She had a soft spot for him or, as he saw it, she thought he was a soft touch.

'See if you can head her off.'

Kersey went downstairs. 'You're too late, Ella. It was all over this morning. No more briefings until the result of the autopsy.'

Ella brushed past him. 'Don't give me that crap, Fido. Where is he?'

She glanced round the room, where two uniformed men and a DC were punching their keyboards as though they were fruit machines, then made for the stairs.

'I've nothing for you until this evening, Ella.'

'But I've got something for you.' She looked at Lucy Lane; a few seconds of critical study. 'I see! The squad's answer to equal opportunity; all nicely packaged. Pity she isn't black, you could have killed two birds . . . What do you let her do?'

Wycliffe was roused. 'Cut that, Ella, or I'll have you put out!'

Ella sat down, unruffled. In winter she wore a sheepskin coat that smelt of goat; in summer the smell was of honest-to-God sweat.

'You've got problems, you're adrift. You don't even know if you've got two cases or one. What possible connection is there between Agnes in the freezer and Hilda in the pool? That's what you're asking yourself.'

'You're going to tell me?'

'No, I've no more idea than you have, but I can give you a tip that may or may not be useful. At least the old woman's case is mixed up with the estate of one Henry Rule, late of the city of Plymouth — right?'

'So?'

She fished out a cigarette from the pocket of her cardigan and lit it. 'Last year I did some work on Henry Rule, among other antique dealers, for a series of articles called "Tricks of the Trade" — an exposé of the antiques racket. To bring in Henry Rule was digging a bit far back. The public, bless 'em, like their victims warm, but that can come expensive if you get it wrong. Henry had the advantage of being a plausible rogue and recently dead.' She broke off and tapped ash on the floor. 'There's a whole lot of his stuff stored at Tregelles — right?'

'His house furniture, I believe. But so far, Ella, you haven't told me anything and I've other things to do.'

Ella blew smoke across the table. 'So have I, my friend. Is Bertie Harvey on your little list?'

'He's the dead girl's brother-in-law.'

'You know anything of his background?'

'Before he married into the Clemo family he worked for a firm of fine art auctioneers in Exeter.'

'Lovell and Delbos. But before that he was with Henry Rule; he worked for Henry from the time he left school at sixteen until he was twenty-one when Henry retired and sold up the business. I ferreted that out when I was doing research for my articles. I came down here to see him then, but he's a canny customer for all his waffle and as there was nothing in it for him he had nothing for me. According to what I've heard he was Henry's protégé and he must have known what went on.'

Ella stood up. 'Well, that's it then! I know you've got nothing now but when you have — Ella expects.'

At the door she turned back. 'By the way, Charlie, I like your signboard. Very apt.'

When she had gone Lucy Lane said: 'Is she reliable?'

'She has to be; she survives on horse-trading. Sometimes I think she ought to be in our business.'

Kersey had shown discretion and stayed downstairs during the visit, now he returned. 'What was it this time?'

'Bertie Harvey worked for Henry Rule for five years before going to Lovell and Delbos.'

Kersey screwed up his features, a sign of cerebration. 'I wonder what that means?' He can't have thrown up his job in Exeter, come down here, and married Alice, all to get an inside view of domestic life at Tregelles.'

'At least we're gathering ammunition for a heart to heart.'

Wednesday evening

When Wycliffe arrived home after his conference at headquarters, dusk was beginning to close over the estuary and the navigation lights twinkled through a thin mist. Helen had spent most of the day working in the garden and her skin was brown and smooth.

'Sherry?'

They took their drinks into the garden and made a tour of inspection in the fading light.

'I took a chance and cut back the elaeagnus pretty hard . . . It was hollow in the middle, so it's kill or cure . . .'

Wycliffe said: 'I'll try to do the grass at the weekend . . . We shall have to be drastic with the water-lily, you can't see the fish.'

'Talking about the weekend, reminds me; Ruth phoned. She's hoping to come home on Friday for a day or two. Will you be free at all?'

Ruth, his daughter. That very morning he had seen the body of another man's daughter lifted from a quarry pool, wrapped in plastic sheeting, and taken away to the mortuary. What had that girl done which Ruth had not? Why was James Clemo spending this summer evening in despair while he strolled in the warm darkness with his wife and planned their weekend? Who or what decides the who? And the when?

'There's a casserole, it seemed the safest thing; I didn't know when to expect you and you don't usually get much in the way of lunch when you are away.'

At nine o'clock they were drinking coffee and watching the television news. Towards the end of the news a picture of the quarry pool flashed on the screen, followed by another of policemen searching the ground near the quarry edge with, inset, a picture of Hilda.

'A lovely girl!' From Helen.

The newscaster read her piece: 'The body of Hilda Clemo, the seventeen-year-old Cornish girl missing since Saturday, was found this morning in a flooded quarry only a few hundred yards from her home at the caravan park run by her family. Police are treating her death as murder. The quarry pool was searched by a police frogman yesterday and the assumption is that the body was placed in the pool during last night.'

The inset picture expanded to take up the whole screen and Hilda Clemo was looking out, smiling her enigmatic smile at the millions of viewers.

'Police are anxious to hear from anyone who saw Hilda or who knows anything of her movements after four o'clock on Saturday afternoon.'

Helen shivered. 'It brings it home! Sometimes I wonder how you can carry on.'

Franks telephoned at the beginning of the weather forecast: 'About your girl, Charles. What a waste! Lovely creature! Well, I can give you a run-down. What do you want to know?'

'When she died, for a start.'

'You've got a one-track mind, Charles. You know perfectly well I can't answer that.'

'The fact that she was alive on Saturday afternoon between four and five should help.'

'It sets an upper limit, but the point is I've no idea of the conditions under which the body was kept before it was put into the water. Putrefaction is at an early stage and its progress would have been slowed down by immersion. Those quarry pools are usually bloody cold and your local chap gave this one seven degrees when they fished her out. Incidentally, I agree with him that she was probably in the water less than twelve hours.'

'So?'

'Well, assuming the body had been kept out of doors in the shade, or in a cool shed of some sort, she could have died on Saturday, shortly after she went missing. On the other hand, if it was exposed to higher temperatures then it could have been Sunday or Monday.'

'What about cause of death?'

'Difficult. Your man — Hosking — favoured the crescent-shaped injury to the skull, almost at the junction of the lambdoid and sagittal sutures; mainly because he couldn't find anything else. Even after immersion there are still signs that the wound bled freely and he concluded that it must have been inflicted before death, and probably killed her. I agree that the wound was inflicted before death though it's an odd fact that *post mortem* injuries in that region can bleed very freely. But, leaving all that aside, in ordinary circumstances I wouldn't have expected such an injury to be fatal.'

'How was it caused?'

'My guess would be that somebody took a swipe at her with a hammer — not a very powerful blow.'

'But it was the result of a deliberate attack?'

'In my opinion, yes; it's not the sort of injury one comes by accidentally.'

'Any ideas about the hammer?'

'Smallish, with a circular, flat striking surface.'

'Now, what are these circumstances which were not ordinary?'

Franks was unusually hesitant. 'All I can say is that if she'd been found within a reasonable time after receiving the blow, and taken to hospital, one would have offered heavy odds in favour of her recovery.'

'So you think she was left to die.'

'That's the size of it.'

'What about the marks on her neck?'

'Bruises. They puzzle me; they seem to have been made by somebody's fingers, but they can have played little or no part in her death.'

'And the other injuries?'

'All the significant ones, including the fractures, were incurred *post mortem*, probably when she was tumbled over the quarry edge.'

'Any evidence of sexual intercourse immediately before death?'

'You mean, was she raped? I can't tell you. She was in the water long enough to wash away any direct evidence. There was a certain amount of bruising on the thighs but that's a long way from evidence. I suppose the fact that she was naked suggests a sexual angle.'

'You haven't mentioned her pregnancy.'

'Pregnancy? You were on about it this afternoon, about possible type matching for paternity, but the girl wasn't pregnant.'

Wycliffe felt the ground slipping from under his feet. 'On the morning of the day she went missing she was told by her doctor that she was.'

'Then he was mistaken. She wasn't and never has been.'

'She told her sister — '

'I can't help what she told anybody, Charles; I can only give you the facts. Now, do you want any more?'

Wycliffe was left casting about in a void: 'Don't tell me she was a virgin?'

'No, she'd had a certain amount of sexual experience — limited, I'd say.'

'Anything else?'

'No. I haven't done my microscopy yet so I may have other gems for you, but don't expect much.'

Wycliffe put down the telephone.

The television sound had been switched off but the pictures continued to flit across the screen. Wycliffe looked at them like a man in a dream.

'Franks says she wasn't pregnant and never had been.'

Helen said: 'You forget that all I know about the case is what I've read in the newspapers and heard on the radio. They said nothing about her being pregnant.'

'That's true; only the family knew — or thought they did. It wasn't mentioned in the press briefings to save them unnecessary distress. I wonder what old Hosking knows about it.'

'Hosking?'

'The local GP and police surgeon. She didn't see him, she saw his locum, but there's sure to be a note on her card.'

The red-headed doctor was not pleased to be disturbed. 'This is my private house; my records are at the surgery. What exactly do you want to know?'

'Hilda Clemo visited your locum on the morning of the day she died for the result of a pregnancy test. Later that morning she told her sister that it was positive.'

Hosking was incredulous. 'But that's nonsense! I've seen the report; the girl was no more pregnant than I am.'

'Is it possible that your locum misinformed her?'

'No, it damn well isn't! Young Heath told me about the girl when he was handing over. Said she was coming in again about the missed period that started the scare. Of course she was a strange girl . . .'

'Strange?'

'I've known her literally since birth and I don't know the first thing about her. Her mother died when she was four; I don't suppose that helped. They tell me she was very intelligent but I never got more than "yes" and "no" out of her and felt lucky to get that sometimes.'

Wycliffe settled back in his chair and finished his coffee which had gone cold. 'Why would a girl tell her family she was pregnant when she wasn't, and knew that she wasn't?'

Helen had switched off the television and picked up a book. 'To shock them? To draw attention to herself? To have a weapon against someone?'

'Or out of sheer bloody-mindedness.'

'That's possible too, but it might not be for any of those reasons. I remember when I was a girl trying to imagine what

133

would happen if I kicked over the traces and did this or that. How would the family react? How would my friends? When you're young you think a lot about the impact you have on other people — at least girls do. At the same time you're trying to find out what exactly the rules mean and you're tempted to explore the limits.'

Wycliffe was teasing: 'I knew you when you were seventeen and as my recollection goes you didn't seem anxious to explore any limits then.'

'Just as well, wasn't it? But that didn't stop me wondering what it would have been like if I had.' She said it with a wry grin and for an instant Wycliffe saw again the auburn-haired girl he had fallen in love with, and he was touched by tenderness.

'So Hilda threw a stone into the water just to see where the ripples went?'

'Well, it's possible, isn't it?'

'I suppose so, but whatever her reason for pretending, she disappeared that same day and was found dead — murdered — four days later. Was that because she said she was pregnant? It doesn't seem likely, does it? On the other hand it would surely be too much of a coincidence if the two were totally unconnected.'

'I see what you mean.'

Helen picked up her book, prepared to leave it there. It was unusual for them to discuss his cases in detail; not because of professional scruples, nor because she lacked interest, but because they both recognized the need for a still centre in their lives and that was the role of The Watch House with its half-acre of garden.

He felt restless and ineffective. Too many things had happened in too short a time. He had first heard of Hilda Clemo on Monday morning and it was now only Wednesday evening. His mind was a shifting kaleidoscope of images which defied his efforts to interpret or relate. Two images recurred with monotonous regularity: the old woman's body, shrivelled and grey, petrified in death; and the young girl's, bleached and flaccid, but still retaining the form and semblance of life.

The answer was a book before bed; biography is the best sedative, a dose of proxy living. Wycliffe hoarded his biographies, journals, diaries and published letters, as a hypochondriac hoards his pills; two whole shelves of the big bookcase in the living-room. He pondered his choice, from Shonagon's *Pillow Book* to Liane de Pougy, from Trajan to Tsar Nicholas II; he hesitated over Marie Bashkirtseff but decided that she was for emergencies only.

In the end, with the instinct of a connoisseur, he settled on Pepys. Six pages equal to one Mogadon any day.

Chapter Nine

Thursday morning

Another fine morning. By half-past six Wycliffe was in the kitchen making coffee and toast, pleased with himself for having got so far without disturbing Helen. The radio chattered. Lacking any major crisis or scandal it struggled to breathe life into yesterday's dead bones and arrived, with a certain sense of achievement, at the weather forecast.

'The south-west will start the day fine and dry but a depression will bring rain and gale-force winds to Cornwall early this afternoon, and these conditions will spread rapidly over the whole of southern England to reach London and the south-east by evening.'

He had a ninety-minute drive, a press call at ten, and there were things he wanted to set in train before then.

Helen came downstairs in her dressing-gown.

'Did I wake you?'

'I don't think so. Would you like an egg or something?'

'No, this is fine. There's coffee already made.'

'When shall I see you again?'

'Probably at the weekend.'

'Don't forget Ruth will be home.'

She saw him off. The roads were quiet and he made good time, arriving at the Incident Room by half-past eight. Kersey and Lucy Lane were already in possession. He broke the news.

'I've had Franks's preliminary report: Hilda was not pregnant.'

136

'You mean — '

'I mean that she was told by the doctor on Saturday morning that her pregnancy test was negative.'

Both Kersey and Lucy Lane took time to digest this.

'She must have had some motive . . .'

'What could she gain?'

'I suppose it could have been sheer bloody-mindedness but it could be that she wanted to score off someone, perhaps to have some sort of lever.'

'Surely not Ralph Martin?'

'I think he was a fall-guy, set up for the family. At the moment, the point I want to make is — no word to the press. It has never been stated that she was pregnant so there is no need to say that she wasn't.

'I want you, Lucy, to tell the family.'

'Do I also tell them that she knew she wasn't pregnant?'

'Yes. They're bound to talk to the doctor at some stage. In any case I think they have a right to know.

'Now, anything else?'

Kersey said: 'Old Penrose has no inventory of Henry Rule's stuff at the farm but he's agreed to one being made. I've passed the job to a valuer in St Austell and he'll be up there this afternoon.'

'Make sure we have somebody there. I want this to be official. I'm seeing Innes this morning, but before that we have the press.'

The press briefing was tricky.

'First, I have to tell you that Agnes Rule, whose body was found in a domestic freezer at Tregelles Farm, appears to have died a natural death; there is no suggestion of foul play.'

'Then why was her body put in the freezer?'

'That is under investigation at the moment. When the investigation is complete, appropriate steps will be taken and you will be told about them.'

Like a politician, he had become practised in hiding behind a mask of words.

'About the girl. Have you had the autopsy report?'

'I have had a preliminary report.'

'Was it a sex killing?'

'There is no evidence of the kind of violence usually associated with a sex killing.'

'Was she strangled?'

'No, it seems that the cause of death was a blow to the head.'

'And the motive?'

'If we knew that we should be a good deal nearer finding the killer.'

It went on for half an hour but Wycliffe got away at last and, within minutes, he was driving along the now familiar route out of the village, up the hill past the caravan park and on to the Gorran road. The lane off to Tregelles was unmarked and he almost missed it. The Moyles' place looked derelict and deserted; the car bumped along the rutted lane. He could see the sea, a distant silvery streak under a blue, cloudless sky.

He parked next to the *deux chevaux* in front of the Inneses' house. As before, the door stood wide open. He knocked, but there was no reply. The sleek golden retriever appeared, gave him a disdainful glance, and withdrew. He knocked again and, after an interval, he heard the wheels of Polly Innes's chair. She came into view around the corner of the passage and advanced towards him. She wore the same grey, paint-spattered smock he had seen her in before.

'Oh, Mr Wycliffe! . . . I've no idea where Tristan can be . . . Tristan!' She raised her voice, tense and petulant.

There was no reply, but the sound of a WC flush came from somewhere in the house.

'Do please come in.'

She manoeuvred her chair to push open the drawing-room door before Wycliffe could do it for her. 'If you will sit down . . . Tristan won't be long.' Then: 'Perhaps you will excuse me, there is something I must do in the studio.'

Wycliffe was left alone in the long room with its dark woodwork, discreet Liberty fabrics, and rows of books with mellowed spines. Blue and white porcelain pots gleamed in odd nooks. All was subdued, muted, except for the gem-like luminosity of the Indian miniatures which, here and there, found a place on the walls.

Footsteps in the passage, and Innes came in. His manner was grave. 'Of course we've heard the news . . . Such a tragedy! Polly is terribly shocked.'

Before he could sit down he was followed by his wife in her wheelchair. She had changed her smock for a jade-green tunic which seemed to emphasize her extreme pallor. Wycliffe thought that she must be a very sick woman.

When they were settled Wycliffe said: 'I understand from the reports that neither of you saw or heard anything unusual during the night of Tuesday/Wednesday?'

'Nothing.'

'Forgive me, but do you share a room?'

Mrs Innes said: 'We share a bed.' The words were spiced with aggression.

'Good!' But Wycliffe did not make it clear what it was that had his approval. 'Then I'll come to the point.' He took from his briefcase the sketch diagram found in Hilda's room. 'I suppose I'm consulting you as an expert witness, but first, have you seen this before?' He handed the sketch to Innes.

Innes studied it for some time then passed it to his wife. 'May I?'

'Have you seen it before?'

'No.'

'I suppose that art historians, like others, have their special period — '

Innes interrupted with a smile. 'Mine is nineteenth-century European painting so I should know something about Pissarro, if that is what you were going to ask.'

'Yes, that sketch was found in Hilda's room pinned to the underside of a desk drawer.'

'How very odd! Do you think it was some sort of exercise? I know that she was becoming interested in pictures, particularly in the work of the Impressionists, but why hide it?'

'This letter was with the sketch; you will see that it is dated last January.'

Polly Innes said: 'That was about the time she started coming

139

here.' She was attempting to join in the conversation but she was tense, on edge.

Innes read the letter. 'How extraordinary!'

'You knew nothing of this?'

'Nothing. As we have told you, Hilda was not a confiding person.'

'Did you discuss Pissarro with her?'

'Not more than any of the other Impressionists. You see, Hilda was by no means knowledgeable about paintings but she was learning fast — as she seemed to do in any field that interested her. She was a remarkable girl which makes it all the more tragic that it should all end like this.'

His wife was looking from him to Wycliffe and back again, obviously under great stress. Abruptly, she said: 'You must excuse me, Mr Wycliffe, I'm sorry . . .'

Innes got up and opened the door for her to pass through. When he had closed it behind her he turned to Wycliffe. 'Polly is having a bad spell and this business has upset her. She was very fond of Hilda.'

When they were settled again he said: 'You think that this sketch and letter might have something to do with her death?'

'I don't know, it seems unlikely, but we have to follow every lead. This is something which Hilda saw fit to hide and that, in itself, gives it importance. Can you offer any comment on the sketch?'

'Only to repeat what the chap at the National said in his letter. Hilda's sketch suggests one of the many paintings made by Pissarro in and around the village of Pontoise where he lived for several years, only interrupted by his taking refuge in England during the Franco–Prussian war. It was, incidentally, in England that he got married.'

'Really?' Wycliffe was attentive and deferential. 'I have heard that from time to time catalogues of the known works of notable painters are compiled, indicating where they were to be found at the time of compilation.'

Innes seemed mildly surprised that Wycliffe should be so well informed.

'You are quite right, and at the present time one of the London auction houses is engaged in computerizing a mass of such information which they hope to keep up to date.'

'Indeed! My interest is in any of Pissarro's work which might have been in private hands in the Plymouth area at the outbreak of the last war.'

This very specific statement surprised Innes even more and it was a moment or two before he recovered his poise. 'Then you may be in luck. There is a magnificent, illustrated catalogue, compiled by Pissarro's son, Lucien, and L. Venturi, the critic and art historian: *Camille Pissarro, son art, son oeuvre.* It was published in Paris in 1937. It could be of help. If not, there are other sources.'

After a reflective pause, Innes added: 'If you wish, I will make some enquiries.'

Wycliffe declined the offer. 'Thank you, but no. Now that you have shown me how to set about it I can get the machinery to work and save you the trouble.'

They were interrupted by a scratching at the door; it was pushed open and the retriever padded into the room and settled at his master's feet.

Innes shifted uncomfortably in his chair. 'Your interest arises wholly from Hilda's sketch and her letter to the Gallery?'

'Not wholly.'

There was a lull; it was clear that Innes felt snubbed by Wycliffe's failure to enlarge. He waited for him to resume the conversation — or leave — but Wycliffe gave no sign of doing either, and the silence was beginning to be embarrassing.

Finally Wycliffe asked a question which seemed trivial: 'Are you acquainted with Harvey — Hilda's brother-in-law?'

'I know him as a neighbour; he's been here two or three times and he attended some lectures I gave in St Austell on the precursors of Impressionism.'

'I understand that he worked for a firm of fine art auctioneers in Exeter before he came here.'

Innes was polite. 'Really? He has never mentioned that but

it did occur to me that his interest in art generally had a professional bias.'

'Has he ever asked your opinion about a picture, about any *object d'art*, or antique?'

'No.'

'You have had no contact with him of any sort concerning items stored at Tregelles Farm?'

Innes flushed. The atmosphere had changed. He was being interrogated instead of consulted, and he realized that the whole interview might have been a disguised interrogation.

He became brusque. 'I would like you to understand, Mr Wycliffe, that I have never allowed myself to be associated with any commercial transaction involving buying, selling, or even valuing any object of the kind you describe.'

Wycliffe stood up. 'Thank you, Mr Innes — that is what I wanted to hear.'

As he was moving towards the door he turned. 'By the way, I ought to tell you: the autopsy shows that Hilda was not pregnant.'

Innes had got up from his chair and was following Wycliffe from the room but he stopped short. 'Not pregnant? You mean that she was mistaken?'

'Not even that. Hilda was given the result of a pregnancy test on Saturday morning by Hosking's locum. It was negative.'

'But that is incredible! I can scarcely believe that she would have invented such a story. If she knew it was untrue — ' He broke off. 'How very strange!'

Innes followed Wycliffe out. Wycliffe said: 'Do you mind if I leave my car here? I want to call on the Rules and it's hardly worth driving such a short distance.'

'What? No, of course not! Leave it here by all means.'

He stood watching Wycliffe as he walked off down the lane to the farm and his wife, in her wheelchair, joined him.

Once again Wycliffe was affected by the stillness and the silence. He could see over the low hedges, a seemingly deserted countryside and, in the distance, an empty sea. A rabbit, nibbling grass in the middle of the track, scuttled away only when he was within a few feet. Surely the creature was keeping very late or very early hours? Perhaps it hadn't heard about diurnal rhythms.

He let himself into the farmyard and knocked on the open door. Jane Rule's cracked voice called: 'You can come in.'

She was standing over the stove, gently stirring the contents of a large saucepan. She raised a spoonful to her lips and tasted it. The smell was appealing and his taste-buds were tickled. Did they live on soups and stews?

'Smells good.'

'It is good. You cook it slow and never let it boil.' She spooned some into a cup and handed the cup to him. 'Try it.'

Consorting with suspected criminals? Didn't fat-cat lawyers do it every day?

'Mrs Rule, are you telling the Court that the chief superintendent shared your meal with you?'

But he accepted the soup. In part it was in reaction against the atmosphere he had just left.

God knows what was in it but the soup had a wonderfully satisfying taste and substance.

'Anyway, what are you here for now?'

'Several things, but first may I use your telephone? It's long distance but I'll pay for the call.'

She shrugged and nodded towards the telephone which was bracketed to the wall.

He dialled Directory Enquiries, asked for the number of the Courtauld Institute, then dialled.

He had a double purpose: first, to set the business of the pictures in train, and then to see Jane Rule's reaction — if any.

'The Courtauld? . . . May I speak to Mr David Joyce, please? . . . Chief Superintendent Wycliffe . . .'

David Joyce had been called as an expert witness in the Marcella Tate case, just a year ago.

'Mr Joyce . . . Wycliffe . . . You remember?'

Joyce did remember and Wycliffe explained what he wanted. 'Any Pissarros that were in private hands in the neighbourhood of Plymouth during or shortly after the last war . . . Is there a chance? I mean, I hope I'm not asking too much?'

'It's not asking much for me to look up the Pissarro–Venturi catalogue. That came out in '37 and might help. If that doesn't yield, we'll try other possibles. Over the past fifty years we've got together quite a lot of material on the whereabouts of Impressionist works which we try to update. Leave it to me and I'll call you back this afternoon. I may not have anything for you then but at least I should be able to give you the odds.'

Jane Rule was showing no interest. She had gone back to the stove and was lifting dripping anonymous chunks of something from another saucepan into an enamel bowl, while the cat and dog fawned about her legs.

Wycliffe gave Joyce the Incident Room number.

Joyce said: 'What's the weather like down there?'

'Lovely, at the moment.'

'It's the same here, but I'd swap my roofs with chimney pots for your harbour with fishing boats any day.'

Jane had placed the enamel bowl on the floor, and cat and dog were feeding amicably. Now she was standing by the table, motionless. It was as though she could, at will, achieve a state of suspended animation.

Wycliffe took out his wallet and handed her a note. 'That will cover the cost of the call, thank you.'

She said nothing but she crumpled the note into the pocket of her apron.

'I wanted you to know that Hilda was not pregnant.'

'She made it up?'

'Yes.'

'Ah!'

'You don't seem surprised.'

'That girl couldn't resist stirring.'

'Stirring?'

'She looked for trouble, and where she couldn't find it, she made it. James is a fool and he spoilt her, but I feel sorry for him.'

'You feel sorry for James Clemo? But early Wednesday morning he was arrested in your yard with a shotgun.'

144

'Oh, that!' She was laying places on the table for herself and her son. 'With him it's all bluster; he's always been the same, but with the guts he's got he couldn't shoot a rabbit.'

'Why was he so sure that it was your son who assaulted Hilda?'

She was cutting large chunks of bread from a loaf. She said nothing and Wycliffe persisted: 'Mrs Rule, I am reaching a stage where I have to have answers to certain questions. Whether those answers are connected with my investigation or not, I will decide, but I intend to have them. Why was James Clemo convinced that Clifford raped and murdered his daughter?'

Jane looked up at the little clock, ticking away on the mantelpiece. 'He'll be coming in soon for his meal. He's got no watch but he's never more'n ten minutes out.'

'Mrs Rule!'

Her eyes sought his and she seemed to resign herself. 'All right! You know about Esther?'

'I know that she came to work here when she left school, before the Clemos took her in.'

Jane was smoothing the table-top with a skinny hand. 'Six months after she came here she was assaulted and raped.'

'By your son?'

'That's what they said; that's what they got me to agree to.'

'I don't understand.'

'No. Elinor, James's mother, her that they buried last Friday, she arranged it all.' Jane pursed her lips. 'She was a strong-minded woman.'

'But what had she to do with — '

'It was Gordon — my husband, her brother — who did it . . . She was a skinny little thing and though her mother was what she was, Esther was innocent. She'd carry on like we did, she'd strip to the waist to wash at the sink and not think twice about it . . . But she done it once too often. One day when I was out, Gordon took her. It frightened the poor little thing nearly to death, she couldn't speak for hours. I should've known better than to let her carry on like that.

'Anyway, old man Clemo, James's father, was alive then — and if he'd known it was Gordon he'd 've had us off the farm quicker'n you could say knife. Strict chapel he was; we Rules was always church.'

She sighed. 'So the fault was put on Clifford. Gordon could do no wrong where Elinor was concerned, and she had it all worked out. Clifford was weak in the head so it wouldn't hurt him. Esther's mother, who didn't care tuppence anyway, was squared, and the girl was promised a real home as one of the Clemo family if she kept her mouth shut. When you come to think of it the poor lil' toad didn' have much option, did she?'

'And James Clemo doesn't know this?'

She looked him in the eyes. 'After Elinor died last Friday, Esther and me was the only ones living to know it until this minute. They never told Clifford nothing.' There were heavy footsteps in the yard. 'Here he is. Will all this have to come out now?'

'Why should it?'

'Are you going? There's a man coming from the lawyer this afternoon to make a list of Agnes's stuff.'

'I know. I want to look around her room before I go.'

Jane shrugged. 'I only live here.'

The door opened and Clifford came in. 'Oh!'

'Sit down and have your soup. You can dish it up yourself.'

Wycliffe went upstairs to what had been the old lady's room. The curtains were drawn over the small window so the room was almost in darkness. He drew them back. It all looked much the same as it had done when he was there with Kersey. Only the dummy head with its grey wig was missing.

He had come to look at the pictures. There were four oil paintings of different sizes in swept, gilded frames. He was no authority on paintings but they looked to him like 'furnishing pictures', the frames probably more valuable than the paintings. All four bore signatures but he did not recognize any of them.

He went back downstairs. Clifford was eating his meal but Jane was standing, waiting.

'Have you seen all you want to?' She seemed almost reluctant to let him go and followed him out. They stood, looking at the littered yard, the straw, the manure, the pecking hens, the decaying sheds and rusting machinery.

146

Jane Rule said: 'What will happen to me — about Agnes, I mean?'

'The autopsy showed that she died a natural death.'

'So?'

'You concealed her death in a manner that aggravated the offence. In all the circumstances you'll probably get a suspended sentence, but you must have a lawyer.'

She was silent for a while then she said: 'I shan't last for ever, and what'll happen to him when I'm gone? What will he do?' The questions were rhetorical.

Wycliffe said: 'Has Bertie Harvey ever been in the house — apart from the old dairy?'

'Two or three times, he came to see Agnes with the girl.'

'You mean Hilda?'

'Yes; they two was very thick but it was none of my business.'

'What did they come to see Agnes about?'

'How should I know? It was before she went queer, when she had her own life so to speak. She didn't tell me more'n she had to. Lately I've wondered if she was selling stuff through him — small things.'

'Apart from her visits with Bertie, did Hilda come here often, alone?'

'Often? I dunno about that — once in a month or six weeks maybe.'

'Why did she come? Have you any idea?'

'She didn't come to see me, that's for sure. Once when I went up there for something she seemed to be reading to Agnes, another time she was drawing.'

'*Drawing*?'

'That's what I said. She was doing something with pencil and paper and it wasn't writing.'

'What was she drawing?'

'I never looked to see.'

'And Innes — did he ever come here?'

'He was never in the house to my knowledge but I can't speak for when I was out.'

'Do you go out much?'

'Every Friday I go over to St Austell for my shopping. It's cheaper.'

Wycliffe nodded to the dilapidated Morris Minor. 'You drive over?'

'I don't walk, if that's what you mean; 'tis the best part of eight mile.'

Wycliffe lingered in the sun, as though he too was reluctant to break off contact. It was odd; he felt a perverse admiration for Jane Rule, struggling against the odds, and a kind of kinship. As a boy, living in a remote rural area, he had known other women like Jane, other amiable half-wits like Clifford, other families like the Rules and the Clemos with their loyalties and their feuds, their 'rich' relatives, and their poor dependants.

'Did Agnes show any interest in her pictures?'

'She used to change them sometimes.'

'Change them?'

'With ones that was in store. She was always swapping things around when she was herself. "I think I'll have up that little chest, Jane, this great thing takes up too much room." Clifford and me would've spent half our time humping furniture up and downstairs if she had her way.'

He made up his mind at last and walked back to the car. The Innes place seemed silent and deserted but the *deux chevaux* was still there and the front door was wide open.

Chapter Ten

Thursday afternoon

'Lets go and get some lunch.'

Wycliffe and Kersey walked along the quay and as they reached the wharf the brilliant light was dimmed as clouds building from the south-west obscured the sun.

'Weather's breaking,' Kersey said.

'The Seiners all right with you?'

'Fine.'

A local lad in the Force had commended The Seiners. It was tucked away inconspicuously in an alley and the entrance looked like the way into a private house, so that it was almost emmet-proof. (Emmet = Old English for ant, and modern Cornish for 'summer visitors'.) The landlord's wife was celebrated for her pasties but these had to be ordered in advance so Wycliffe and Kersey had to settle for a helping of the communal beef pie.

Wycliffe ordered a lager for himself and a bitter for Kersey. 'That soup made me thirsty.'

'What soup?'

'Never mind.'

They found a tile-topped table for two in a corner by a window that was little wider than an arrow slit. The locals preferred to huddle around the bar, many of them stood, pasty in hand. There was a hubbub of chat and the occasional burst of laughter, so it was possible to talk, and nobody was interested. Wycliffe brought Kersey up to date.

'You think this picture business might lead somewhere?'

'I've no idea. We are investigating a murder and looking for a

149

motive. Hilda was enquiring about a Pissarro painting and trying to keep her interest in it to herself. Where did she see it? Franks says that Henry Rule made a packet acquiring the contents of blitzed properties during the war, and out of newly impoverished and gullible old ladies afterwards. It seems that some of his acquisitions bordered on theft. It might be useful to find out whether any of Pissarro's works were in Henry's catchment area at the time.'

'Surely he'd have unloaded them long ago?'

'I don't know, pictures in that category are dangerous goods unless you have access to the underground market, and Rule had already burned his fingers once or twice.'

It was beginning to rain. Through the little window Wycliffe could see fat drops making dark splashes on the cobbles. 'Have you ever thrown a stone into a pool and watched the ripples?'

Kersey knew his Wycliffe and was equal to him. 'I think I can remember something of the sort, sir.'

'If you throw in two or three, a few feet apart, you get more fun but it's a bit of a mess where the ripples meet and interact, cancelling or deflecting each other.'

'I must try it sometime. You think someone has been throwing stones into our pool?'

'I'm sure of it. All I'm saying is that we mustn't fall into the trap of looking for one solution to two, or even three problems.'

'You don't think it's time we started turning the screw a bit on the obvious candidates?'

'We're not ready. When we start we must know exactly where we are going.'

Kersey emptied his glass. 'Will you have another?'

'I'd prefer a coffee.'

They had to run the gauntlet of the rain back along the North Quay to the Incident Room. Potter, the fat DC, was duty officer. 'Miss Esther Clemo is upstairs with DS Lane, sir.'

Wycliffe went upstairs. Lucy Lane was sitting at the desk, her back to the window; Esther was perched, bolt upright, on a chair by the desk. She wore a navy-blue gaberdine mackintosh like a schoolgirl's, and a once stylish toque which she must have rescued from a wedding. Her forehead was decorated with sticking plaster and it was obvious that she had a bandage on her gloved right hand.

'Miss Clemo has come to give us some information, sir.'

Esther was uneasy. 'I went to the priest and he told me that it was my duty. I only hope he was right.'

Wycliffe signalled to Lucy Lane to continue and took a chair near the door.

They waited.

'You don't need me to tell you that James made a fool of himself on Tuesday night. I was afraid he might do something silly and when I woke up in the early morning I had a feeling . . . He'd been in such a state that evening — and he'd been drinking. Anyway, I looked in his room and he wasn't there. He wasn't in his office either and his gun was missing, so I went after him.' She broke off with a small gesture.

'You knew, or guessed where he'd gone?'

'I knew all right! Anyway, I went up through the park and through the trees, then as I was passing the quarry pool, I heard a loud splash.' She paused, disturbed by the recollection. 'I couldn't for the life of me make out what it could be. I waited, and almost turned back, but nothing else happened so I went on.

'When I got to the stile into the farmyard I heard a commotion. It was James and the policeman, then Jane Rule joined in so I knew it was all right. I mean he hadn't done anything. I never really thought he would but — ' The blue eyes sought Lucy's in concern. 'James's bark is always worse than his bite but, upset like he was — and, like I said, he'd been drinking — I couldn't be sure . . .'

She brought her hands together against her flat chest. 'First I was for going into the yard with the others and getting him out of it, but I didn't want to make things worse; I know what he is, so I started back. I forgot to say it was very foggy. Anyway, when I reached where the path leads off round the top of the quarry I saw a man standing on the path. He must have been ten yards or so from me.' She shuddered. 'I was frightened, I'm not sure why I was so frightened. I mean, I didn't know then what he'd done, but there it was. I ran down the track and back through the trees . . .' She raised her hand to her forehead. 'That was when I fell down and did this.'

'You're sure it was a man?'

She frowned. 'Yes, but I couldn't tell you why.'

'Was he tall or short, thin or fat?'

'He wasn't fat, but what with the mist and the dark . . . I think he must have been fairly tall.'

'Is that what you came to tell us, Miss Clemo?'

She took a deep breath. 'No, not all. I wish it was.' She was distressed.

Lucy Lane said: 'Take your time, Miss Clemo.'

She nodded. 'When I got back into the house I went up to my room and I noticed that Bertie's door was a bit open. I don't know why, but it made me wonder . . . Anyway, I went into his room . . . He wasn't there, his bed hadn't been slept in.'

Wycliffe spoke for the first time: 'This was yesterday morning, Miss Clemo. You must have seen him since. Have you said anything to him?'

She turned to look at Wycliffe, incredulous. 'There was nothing I could say.'

'No, perhaps not, but has anything about him or his behaviour made you think that he may be aware of your suspicion?'

She made an impatient movement. 'Can you imagine what it's like in that house with everything that's happened since Friday, when we buried Granny Clemo?'

'I'm sorry.'

'We don't look at each other, let alone speak if we can help it.'

The telephone rang. Lucy Lane answered. 'Mr Joyce for you, sir; Courtauld Institute.'

'I'll take it downstairs.' He turned to Esther. 'If you will excuse me . . .'

Joyce said: 'I've got something for you but whether it's what you want is another matter. Have you ever heard of Alleston Manor?'

'I've heard of it but I can't place it at the moment.'

'It's somewhere on your patch — on the Tamar, a few miles from Plymouth, I think. Anyway we have a record, dated 1937, of two Pissarros in the possession of the Honourable Mrs Melville-Treece at Alleston Manor. I haven't a clue what happened to them, but we have reproductions which are not too bad for the time.'

'Can you give me titles?'

'Yes. One is *The Village of Pontoise*, and the other, *Fruit Trees at the Hermitage*, both painted in the same year — 1876 — and both oil on canvas.'

'Sizes?'

'The first, eighteen inches by twenty-one; the second, twenty-four inches by twenty-eight.'

'What does the first look like?' Wycliffe was making notes.

'Village street, cottages, larger houses, trees, farm carts and figures. He painted several that were somewhat similar.'

'Sounds promising. Would it be possible to send me a photocopy? Colour doesn't matter at this stage.'

'No problem. I'll put it in the post tonight.'

As a schoolboy studying biology, Wycliffe had shaken samples of soil with water in glass cylinders and watched the turmoil of suspended particles of all sorts and sizes. Then, with a pinch of lime added, in a remarkably short space of time, order would begin to appear out of chaos as the particles settled into beautifully graded layers. Something like that seemed to happen in some of his cases and he felt now that he might just have been handed that pinch of lime.

He went back upstairs.

'Miss Clemo has been telling me — ' Lucy and Esther seemed to have established a rapport.

'I was telling Miss Lane that Bertie was far too familiar with Hilda but I can't believe that he killed her; he always seems to me a weak, not a violent man, but there's no knowing what will happen between a mature man and a girl like Hilda.'

'Like Hilda?'

Esther shook her head. 'She was perverse, there's no denying that, and when a young girl realizes her power over men but she

153

hasn't got the sense to see its dangers — ' She broke off and, to Wycliffe's astonishment, tears were coursing down her pale cheeks. 'I'm sorry . . . I only hope I've done the right thing.'

'You can be sure of that. We have to have all the facts and it's up to us to sort them out.'

'Then I hope you will, for all our sakes.'

'Just one more question, Miss Clemo: the figure you saw through the mist, do you really think it was Bertie?'

She hesitated, frowning. 'I don't know what to say. It could have been but it could have been almost any man. I couldn't see . . .'

Wycliffe said: 'I think we should let it be known that you have been here.'

'But that's just what I don't want! I thought I could come here . . . Father Dole assured me that you wouldn't — '

Wycliffe interrupted: 'I don't want to frighten you, Miss Clemo, but if whoever you saw realizes you have been to the police and made a statement, there will be no point in him taking any steps against you.'

She was agitated. 'You think that he might?'

'We have to make sure that he doesn't. You are willing to make a formal statement?'

She looked at him, weary and frightened. 'I suppose so.'

'If you agree, we will telephone the house and tell them you will be delayed because you are here making a statement.'

She nodded, listless. 'If that's what you think.'

'And one other thing: shouldn't you tell James the truth about what happened years ago when you were at Tregelles?'

She flushed like a girl. 'I've already told him — this morning.' She spoke in little above a whisper. 'He was upset, and he holds it against me.'

'I'm glad you told him. Now Miss Lane will show you to the next room and arrange for someone to take down what you have told us. Afterwards you will be asked to sign it, then we will have you driven back home.

'Would you like a cup of tea — or coffee?'

She nodded. 'Tea, please.'

Lucy took her away, leaving Wycliffe thoughtful. He was often depressed by the sadness he found about him, especially amongst women. In a way Esther and Jane Rule were in the same boat, they belonged to a breed of women who were either unaware of, or disillusioned by their sex, their affection always blunted by its target.

He went downstairs, feeling restless. A mixed bag of DCs and PCs were at the keyboards, nourishing the computer with titbits from the lives of people, some of whom had never heard of Hilda Clemo until she became a news item on the television. Kersey was standing, looking out of the shop window. It had been covered half-way up with brown paper to discourage spectators.

The wind was rising in gusts which swept curtains of rain over the grey sea, over the harbour, and on to the gleaming, grey roofs of the clustered houses. It was no longer a toy-town fishing village for the tourist; in a strange way it seemed to have recovered its identity and its dignity.

Kersey said: 'I've just taken a call from a ward sister at Truro City Hospital. One of her patients thinks he saw Hilda Clemo on Saturday afternoon, near Tregelles. It seems he's a rod-and-line, shore-fishing buff, and he was on his way to his favourite slippery rock near Pabyer Point. Do you think we should send someone down?'

'How did he get himself into hospital?'

'An RTA on Sunday night, his car climbed the hedge and he was badly knocked about; only now able to sit up and take notice.'

'Yes, better get somebody down there. Send Lucy when she's finished upstairs.'

Wycliffe turned to Potter who, as usual, had a mug of tea at his elbow. 'Look in the phone book for Melville-Treece. Could be the Honourable Mrs, but I'm not sure if she's still with us. Last known address, Alleston Manor.'

PC Richards, one of the local lads, spoke up. 'Excuse me, sir, there's a Mrs Melville-Treece, a very old woman, who lives with her daughter up Heligan way, just a couple of miles from the village. Stanley House, it's called. I think she or her family used to have Alleston Manor.'

Potter had found her in the phone book. 'Here we are, sir; "Melville-Treece, the Hon. Mrs M., Stanley House — "'

'See if you can get her on the phone and ask her if she'll see me in the next half-hour.'

It was arranged.

Wycliffe got PC Richards to drive him, a fresh-faced youth who looked as though he should still be at school. Policemen really were getting younger, dammit! 'How long have you been in the Force, Richards?'

'Three years, sir; I'm twenty-two.'

Twenty-two. Wycliffe had been going out with Helen for five years when he was twenty-two, and they were planning to get married.

'Are you married?'

'Hope to be next year, sir.'

Stanley House stood four-square with no nonsense and little charm, built by some hard-headed Cornishman who had made his money out of china clay, or tin, or copper, early in the last century. It fronted on a balustraded terrace and a lawn, surrounded by rhododendron thickets and bounded by a screen of trees. When he stood on his terrace and surveyed his domain he must have felt that he had arrived. Now he and his family had long gone.

'How can I help you, Chief Superintendent?'

The Honourable Mrs Melville-Treece, at eighty-eight, was upright and ambulant, not to say spry. Her voice was a trifle cracked, but she spoke with that incisive and precise enunciation which has become a badge of the Royals.

Wycliffe explained what he wanted, and hoped that the old lady was as indulgent as she was courteous.

'You see, Mr Wycliffe, the old house at Alleston Manor was destroyed by enemy action during the war. It was during one of the night bombing raids on Plymouth. A German bomber being chased, so they said, by night fighters, unloaded its bombs at random and one came down in the yard behind the house. The back of the house was totally destroyed, though the front was untouched. However, architects advised me that any rebuilding would have to be total and that was out of the question. The old house was too big for us anyway.'

She smiled. 'I recall that I was in the small drawing-room with my daughter, Gwendoline, when the bomb dropped and we were listening to the comedian, Tommy Handley, on the wireless.'

Gwendoline, now a plump, matronly woman in her fifties, hovered and smiled but spoke little.

Above the fireplace there was a 'Bloomsbury' portrait of mother and infant daughter.

Wycliffe said: 'The Pissarros — I understand that there were two of them?'

'Yes, indeed, and looking back I realize they were potentially our most valuable possessions from a pecuniary point of view. At the time I did not see them as very important. They had been in the family for many years; my paternal grandfather bought them when he was attached to the embassy in Paris, sometime in the late seventies or early eighties of the last century.'

It was the sort of conversation to be had over cups of China tea in Royal Worcester cups, with Osborne biscuits to nibble. But there was something incongruous about the room; it reminded Wycliffe of a vestry in a Methodist chapel; the furniture, an eclectic assemblage, obviously comprising valued pieces from the old house, now looked as uncomfortable as lots in a saleroom. And the gloom outside was no help; water cascaded down the window-panes, and the light was steely grey.

Mrs Melville-Treece went to a nest of bookshelves and, putting on her spectacles, selected a magazine which she opened and handed to Wycliffe. 'Here is an article published in June 1939. It is really about the old house but the Pissarro pictures are featured there.'

The article was one of a series: 'The Smaller Country Houses of England. Alleston Manor — Number 19.' It referred to the house as 'a perfect example of late eighteenth-century small-scale domestic architecture'. There were photographs of the exterior and of the more important rooms, with colour pictures of some of its contents, including the two Pissarros.

'You may borrow the magazine if you wish.'

It seemed to Wycliffe that one of the pictures might well have been the original of Hilda's sketch.

'Were the pictures destroyed in the bombing?'

'Indeed they were not! The big drawing-room was scarcely damaged. But on the night of the bombing we were advised to move out of the house at once and we went to a cousin of mine. The authorities arranged for a guard on the house and so it remained for, oh, several days, at least. People were rightly more concerned about the carnage in the city. At any rate, when the experts arrived to assess the damage, the Pissarros were missing. The police did what they could but, there again, they had more important things to occupy their time.'

'And you've heard nothing of them since?'

'Nothing, until your visit this afternoon. Do you think it possible that they may be recovered?'

Wycliffe was cautious. 'It seems unlikely; indeed, their connection with my case is, at most, tenuous, and may be non-existent. Just one more question: do you have any recollection of an antiques dealer called Rule? He had his shop in Queen Mary Street.'

Her expression quickened. 'Henry Rule? Of course I remember him! When my husband was alive (my husband was in the RNVR and he was killed in the early months of the war), we did quite a lot of business with Henry. Later, he was a pillar of strength in all the problems arising from our bomb. As a matter of fact it was he who found us this house.'

Mrs Melville-Treece was too well bred to ask questions and Wycliffe did his best to respond to the old lady's courtesy and charm. They parted with expressions of mutual goodwill.

Back in the car Wycliffe compared the magazine reproduction of the Pontoise street scene with a photocopy of Hilda's sketch and decided that she must have had access either to the original picture or to a reproduction.

The young policeman acting as his chauffeur, asked: 'Back to the Incident Room, sir?'

Wycliffe hesitated. 'No, Tregelles Farm. Do you know where it is?'

The wind was still rising and from the top of the hill they were looking out over the bay where a leaden sea was streaked with white.

There was a car already parked in the lane outside Tregelles and Wycliffe remembered the valuer making his inventory. Jane Rule was surprised to see him back so soon but she was almost welcoming. 'What is it now?'

He showed her the two colour reproductions in Mrs Melville-Treece's magazine. 'Have you ever seen a picture like either of these before?'

She opened a drawer of the kitchen table and came out with a pair of spectacles which she put on. They transformed her face, giving it a sudden dignity.

She studied the reproductions then pointed to one of them with her forefinger. 'I've seen that one.'

It was the Pontoise street scene.

'You're sure?'

She nodded. 'I don't take much account of pictures as a rule but I liked that one. It was, well . . . pretty. Agnes had it hanging over her bed for a long time. It was in a nice frame, just like the one in the picture.'

'What happened to it?'

Jane Rule shrugged. 'What's the good of asking me? I told you she was for ever changing things round. It could be out in the old dairy now for all I know.'

'When, approximately, was it hanging in her bedroom?'

She took off her spectacles. 'Before she went queer, anyway. A year ago, perhaps.'

Sounds of furniture being shifted came from the old dairy. 'While I'm here I'll have a word with the valuer.'

Jane tossed her head. 'Three of 'em out there; two to do the work and the other to watch — and one of your lot. You can go through the kitchen if you like.'

He did, and noticed the patch on the floor where the freezer had stood. Now it was in the hands of forensic specialists and much good it would do them.

Mr Tresidder, the valuer, was a stocky Cornishman, well laid back, and inclined to be amused by it all. 'There's some decent stuff here; a good thing the place seems to be dry.'

His two assistants were moving furniture about like pieces on a chequers board in order to reach the rest. Nothing could be taken outside because of the rain.

A uniformed policeman looked on.

'Have you been through the pictures?'

A shrug. 'Nothing much there — some of the frames would fetch a bit.'

'No lost Impressionists?'

A polite chuckle. 'Jane should be so lucky! I suppose it all comes to her?'

'I really don't know what will happen to it. Will you show me how the pictures are stored?'

If the valuer wondered at Wycliffe's interest he made no comment. There were two crates with open tops, one for the smaller, and one for the larger pictures. In the crates the frames stood on edge with layers of felt between.

'You can see the list if you want to.' Tresidder removed two sheets from his file and handed them to Wycliffe. 'Edwardian wall-covering, and not very special at that. As I say, he must have bought them for the frames.'

It was 16.45 by the digital clock in the Incident Room, almost exactly five days since Hilda had walked off the *Sea Spray* when Ralph Martin was about to land his passengers for their Cornish cream teas. No pleasure boats had put to sea today; the quays and the harbour were deserted except for those boatmen engaged in moving craft from the outer to the inner harbour in case the gale worsened.

Wycliffe joined Kersey in the upstair room. 'I think we've got as far as we can. Is Lucy back yet?'

'Not yet. Are you intending to make a move now?'

160

'Tomorrow morning. We shall need a scenes-of-crime team standing by and I want our frogman to make another search of the quarry pool — this time for anything that might have been used to transport the body.'

They talked until Lucy Lane arrived back from her interview with the injured man.

'Poor chap, he's pretty badly knocked about; his car climbed the hedge when he swerved to avoid a straying cow.'

'Don't tell us what he had to say.' Kersey, being Kersey.

'It doesn't amount to a lot but it's odd. He was on his way to the cliffs, down the lane to Tregelles and the footpath. As he reached the Innes place he saw Hilda — he knew her by sight — walk up to the front door, which was open. The dog came out, making a fuss of her, and she went in with the dog.'

'He's saying she was alone?'

'Yes.'

'She didn't knock?'

'Not according to him.'

'And the time?'

'He was vague about time but thought it was "about five".'

'Was the *deux chevaux* there?'

'I'm afraid I didn't ask that.'

'Then get on to the ward sister and ask her to ask him.'

It was a lengthy business, with the ward sister feeling that she had something better to do than run errands, but the answer came eventually: 'He says the *deux chevaux* was not there. He was accustomed to seeing it there and noticed that it had gone.'

During the night the gale strengthened and several times Wycliffe was awakened by the buffeting of the wind causing the hotel building to shudder. Towards dawn it eased but, at seven o'clock, when he looked out of his bedroom window, it was still raining, the sky was leaden and the crests on the still turbulent sea were of dazzling white. Waves smashed against the southern breakwater, sending up sheets of spray.

Chapter Eleven

Wycliffe held an early briefing with Kersey, Lucy Lane and Dixon. In their candid moments research scientists admit that the decision to publish is a critical one: have they really got enough data to support their conclusions in the face of criticism? The criminal investigator has a similar difficulty, he has to be sure that, by showing his hand, he will neither offer the criminal a loophole, nor transgress the rules of procedure so that he ends up with egg on his face and an acquittal on technical grounds.

The four, with Kersey driving, made their way to the caravan park. Rain was driven before a strong south-easterly — a grey wind which bleached the colour from land and sea. There would be many more fine, warm days but they would be autumn days; summer had gone for another year.

It was nine o'clock and people were on the move between their tents and caravans and the toilet blocks; some carried umbrellas which were difficult to control, others held sheets of plastic over their heads. The grass and the roadways were littered with leaves and even twigs, torn from the trees.

Wycliffe went to Reception and spoke to the young girl on duty. She was naively helpful, which seemed out of keeping with an excess of lipstick and eye-shadow, and an ethnic hair-do.

'Is Mr Harvey about?'

'Are you . . .?'

'Chief Superintendent Wycliffe.'

'I thought so. Bertie's up in his office in the Recreation Centre; I spoke to him on the phone just now.'

'And Mrs Harvey?'

'She phoned too; she's coming across later.' She added, lowering her voice: 'I think she's having trouble with her father. He thought the world of Hilda, you know — spoilt her. Now he's in a terrible state.'

They drove up through the park and found Bertie in his office, next to the room where sports gear was hired to customers. It was Wycliffe's first face-to-face encounter with him.

'Mr Harvey? Mr Albert Harvey?'

'That's me or, if you prefer it, I am he.' A compulsive droll but not looking the part just now; his sallow skin was unnaturally pale and his eyes were dark with tiredness. He was sitting at his desk, back to the window, and there were papers everywhere, but Wycliffe felt sure that he had been sitting brooding when they arrived.

'We want to talk to you, Mr Harvey.'

Harvey looked from Wycliffe to the other three and made some attempt at banter. 'All four of you? I doubt if my seating accommodation will run to it.'

'DS Lane and DC Dixon would like to take a look around the premises.'

A sudden stiffening. 'You mean a search? Have you got a warrant?'

'No, but I'm sure Mr Clemo would give his permission. If you are in doubt you had better ring him.'

'I see; so it doesn't matter what I say.'

Lucy Lane and Wycliffe exchanged glances and she left, with Dixon following.

'They will do the outside premises first.'

Wycliffe was in no hurry. He seemed to be taking stock of the office where the only unusual feature was the collection of framed photographs of children on the walls.

Harvey, still battling, said: 'My shop window.'

'Where were you employed before you came here, Mr Harvey?'

'With a firm of auctioneers in Exeter.'

'Lovell and Delbos, the fine art auctioneers?'

'You know, so why ask?'

'And before that?'

'I suppose you know that too. I worked for Henry Rule at his shop in Queen Mary Street, Plymouth.'

'For how long?'

'From the time I left school until he retired.'

'About five years?'

'About that.'

Kersey said: 'I suppose it was a useful apprenticeship in the crooked side of the business, especially when you came to set up deals on your own account.'

Harvey flushed. 'I don't know what you're talking about!' It was a commendable effort at indignation.

Wycliffe was soothing. 'Anyway, with all that experience you must feel pretty much at home in the world of antiques, particularly in the fine art market.'

'I knew my job.' He was playing with a ball-point, flicking it in and out.

'An odd coincidence that you should come here and marry the great-niece of your first employer.'

Harvey was wary and defensive. 'I came here by chance with a former school-friend when we were having a caravan holiday, touring the coasts of Devon and Cornwall and I happened to meet Alice.'

'When did you discover her connection with Henry Rule?'

'Not for several weeks. I used to come down for the odd weekend now and then and it cropped up in casual conversation. Anyway, why should I have been all that interested?'

'A good question, Mr Harvey, but we'll come to that later.' Wycliffe reached into his brief-case and came out with a photograph of the nude Bertie found in Hilda's room. 'Perhaps you can tell us how Hilda got hold of this?'

Harvey's astonishment was real enough and it was a moment or two before he decided how to cope. Then, with an embarrassed laugh, and man-to-man candour, he said: 'It was a damn silly joke.'

Kersey thrust out his lower lip. 'Funny sort of joke to have with your wife's young sister.'

'You think so? Perhaps you're right. The fact is I was thinking of taking up photography as a full-time occupation.' A bleak look round the little office. 'A chance to get out of this! Anyway, I wanted to try my hand at some nude studies and I asked Hilda to pose for me. She said she would if I let her take one of me first.'

'And did she keep to the bargain?'

'Do women ever? No, she backed out.'

Wycliffe shook his head. 'Ingenious but improbable, Mr Harvey. Good lies are always simple.' He reached again into his brief-case. 'But we'll come back to photographs; let's talk about paintings. Look at this!' He handed over the sketch Hilda had made of the Pissarro painting. 'That is a photocopy; the original was found in Hilda's room. Have you seen it before?'

Harvey looked at the sketch. 'No.'

'Nor this?' A photocopy of the letter from the National Gallery.

Harvey took the letter and glanced through it mechanically. 'No, it's very odd, though.'

'Do you know anything of the circumstances in which Hilda did this?'

'No.'

Wycliffe took back the photocopies and Kersey said: 'Careful, Mr Harvey, there are several prints on the letter and the sketch; now yours are on the photocopies.'

Harvey's hands were clasped in front of him on the desk. He was putting on a good front but the strain was showing. 'Do you think I would have let her do that if she'd asked me first? It's obvious that nobody could give an opinion about a picture from a sketch.'

Wycliffe said: 'I'm not suggesting that she consulted you beforehand, but did she show you the reply?'

He was staring down at the top of his desk, his thin face drawn, his cheeks hollowed by shadows, but he managed a rueful grin.

'In view of everything, I don't have much choice, do I? Yes, she did show me the letter.'

'How did she explain what she had done?'

'She said she had seen a picture like it — an oil painting — and she wanted to know if it was genuine and what it was worth.'

'I wonder where she could have seen it?' Kersey, innocent.

'She wouldn't say, and I told her that without seeing the original I couldn't help her.'

Wycliffe said: 'So after a little persuasion she took you along to Agnes Rule's room to show you the picture hanging on the wall.'

Harvey sat back in his chair. 'Walk into my parlour said the spider to the fly.'

Wycliffe was casual. 'We are not inviting you into any trap, Mr Harvey, there's no need. We know that you made at least two visits to Agnes Rule, with Hilda, at that time. Agnes sometimes changed her pictures around and those removed were stored in the old dairy. When she became senile and Jane Rule began to dispose of items of furniture to pay for the old lady's keep, you had access to that store. Think it over, Mr Harvey.'

There was a long pause. The only sounds came from the seemingly frantic ticking of Harvey's little clock and the beating of the rain against the window. Shimmering through the watery panes Wycliffe could see the diving-board rising above the swimming-pool, a ghostly constructivist sculpture.

Wycliffe was the first to speak. 'We now know precisely which picture we are talking about — the one of which Hilda made the sketch.'

He produced the magazine with the two colour reproductions and got up to lay it, open, on Harvey's desk. 'Both those paintings were in the possession of Mrs Melville-Treece of Alleston Manor when her house was bombed during the Plymouth blitz.'

Harvey looked at the magazine briefly then pushed it away.

Wycliffe went on: 'In the confusion following the air-raid, these pictures were stolen and they've never seen since. The Melville-Treece family had a lot of dealings with Henry Rule and he played a large part in clearing up immediately after the bombing of the Melville-Treece house. Now it seems that one of those pictures turned up among his effects only to disappear again . . .'

Kersey leaned forward and brought his face close to Harvey's. 'What happened to it, Mr Harvey? Any ideas?'

Harvey was staring at the papers on his desk. In a low voice he said: 'All right! Hilda told me about the picture after she failed to get help from the Gallery and I went to see it with her. I went a couple of times, sounding out the old lady, but she wouldn't consider parting with it.' He broke off, protesting: 'I had a perfect right to try! As far as I knew the picture was hers to do as she liked with.' He looked from one to the other of the two policemen as though seeking some hint of agreement.

Wycliffe said: 'So what happened?'

'Nothing happened as far as I was concerned. The old lady went queer, Hilda stopped going there, and that was that.'

'And you put it clean out of your mind; you didn't even approach Jane during your negotiations over furniture?'

He hesitated. 'I did mention it and she said she had no idea what had happened to the picture. Of course, she was lying.'

'So you checked over the stuff in the old dairy just in case.'

Harvey said nothing.

Dixon came in and stood, waiting. Kersey turned to glare at him. Wycliffe said: 'All right, Dixon, go through.'

Harvey watched the detective go into his darkroom and close the door behind him. 'What's he looking for in there? Don't I have the right to know what he's looking for?'

Wycliffe was smooth. 'I thought you knew already. He's looking for two paintings worth anything up to half a million, but he is also looking for something much more important: for evidence of where Hilda's body was kept for four days; for the clothes she was wearing when she disappeared; for her shoulder-bag, and for anything else that might establish the motive for her killing and help to identify her murderer.'

Harvey leaned forward in his chair, shaken: 'You can't think that I — '

'Why not? Let's suppose that you've been lying to us; let's

suppose that the picture has already been hived off through one of the dubious connections you made when you were working for Lovell and Delbos. Or that you have it hidden, waiting for the chance . . . If Hilda found out and threatened you . . .'

'But I've told you the absolute truth!' His voice broke and his features were contorted as though he might burst into tears.

Once again there was an interruption from Dixon; he stood in the doorway of the darkroom like a sentinel and, at a sign from Wycliffe, Kersey joined him. The darkroom door closed behind the two men.

Wycliffe and Harvey were left alone. Harvey waited, not trusting himself to speak. His hands were tightly clenched and there were little beads of sweat on his forehead.

When Wycliffe spoke he had changed the subject and his manner was almost conversational. He had discovered long since that abject fear in a suspect can arouse a latent sadism in the interrogator and he would have no part of it. Choose a new angle. 'Surely, Mr Harvey, you must know that a homosexual relationship between consenting adults is no longer an offence?'

Harvey looked up, startled.

Wycliffe went on: 'Hilda found out about your homosexual relationship. That's what the nude photograph meant, wasn't it?'

Harvey remained silent for a while, then he spoke in a low voice. 'Whatever I say — '

Wycliffe cut in: 'Whatever you say, providing it is the truth, is more likely to help you than otherwise.'

He began fiddling with the papers on his desk. 'All right, yes. She came to me one day with a photograph.' He nodded towards the darkroom. 'She must have found it in there, though God knows when; I never allow anyone to go in there . . .' His voice failed him.

'Was it the photograph I showed you just now?'

He shook his head. 'No, she let me keep the one she brought . . . She said it was the only one but, of course, she lied . . .'

Very quietly, Kersey slipped back into the room and took his seat.

'What, do you think, was her motive?'

Harvey made a vague, tired gesture. 'With Hilda it was always the same. She wanted to *know* . . . She wanted to know everything . . . She couldn't bear to think that people had secrets . . . She wasn't even interested, but if she suspected that anybody was trying to hide something from her she wouldn't rest until, one way or another, she'd found out what it was.'

A kind of petulance was giving him the strength. Wycliffe remembered Alice's words: 'In some ways Bertie is still a child himself.' And here he was complaining as a child complains of his playmate.

'And then? What did she do when she knew?'

He spread his hands. 'Nothing. She just let you know — that she knew. That was enough for her.'

'The photograph she returned, was it also of you?'

He did not answer.

'Perhaps of you, with your partner?' Wycliffe looked at Kersey and Kersey nodded. 'With Innes?'

Harvey flushed, and turned on Kersey in a sudden blaze of temper: 'Yes! You know, don't you? You've been in there gloating with the other one!'

Kersey said nothing and Wycliffe went on: 'The two of you spent some nights here?'

Harvey was still excited. 'Is it any of your business? You said yourself — '

Wycliffe became harsh: 'We are not investigating your sex life, Mr Harvey, but murder; the murder of a young girl for whom you pretended to feel affection. I will decide the questions you are asked and form my judgements according to your answers or your refusal to answer. So, do you spend nights here with Innes?'

He shook his head. 'When we have a night together, it's always in one of the empty vans.'

'What about Tuesday night? The night Hilda's body was pushed into the quarry pool? Your bed hadn't been slept in at five in the morning.'

Fear was returning, and his words were barely audible. 'I was in one of the vans.'

169

'Which?'

'B7 on the far side of the site.'

'With Innes?'

'No, Tristan wasn't with me. We had an arrangement but he wasn't able to keep it.'

'Did you leave the van during the night?'

'No, I did not!'

Wycliffe stood up. 'Very well. After he has finished here, Mr Kersey will ask you to allow his men to search your room at the house, and you will be invited to make a written statement concerning this interview.'

Harvey remained seated, staring at the disorderly array on his desk.

Wycliffe left Kersey and Dixon with Harvey. By arrangement, Lucy Lane was waiting for him in the car. The police radio babbled in staccato bursts.

'Scenes of crime?'

'All laid on, sir.'

Lucy Lane was driving; Wycliffe never did so if there was anyone else to do it for him.

They had to make the broad circuit by road, back through the caravan park, up the hill to the main road.

Wycliffe was silent, apparently morose, but Lucy Lane risked a question. 'Any progress with Bertie, sir?'

'He admits to knowledge of the one picture but to nothing else.'

'Has he involved Innes?'

'Only as his homosexual partner.'

'Oh! I see.' But she did not say what it was that she saw.

Another interval and she tried again: 'Hilda went to the doctor for a pregnancy test. We know that it was negative but she must have had a reason for going.'

'You mean there must have been a man and, if it wasn't the Martin boy, then who was it? I see what you're getting at but the fact that Innes and Harvey have a homosexual relationship doesn't exclude them.'

'No, I suppose not.' And with that she seemed content.

They turned off, down the lane past the Moyles' place. The wind had eased but it was still raining hard. Brown water seeped through the hedges from the fields, flooding the track so that their wheels swished through pools and bumped over hidden ruts. There was no fog, but the south-easterly wind bleached colour and definition from the landscape, propagating a universal, misty gloom.

Lucy Lane parked near the *deux chevaux*. For once the Innes front door was closed.

'Wait for me.' Wycliffe walked up to the front door and knocked. After a moment or two, it was opened by Innes himself.

There had been a subtle change in the man; he looked older and Wycliffe could have sworn that there were grey hairs where there had been none before. His manner had changed too, it was as though the veneer of scholarly urbanity had cracked, revealing a man who was unsure of himself, nervous — perhaps truly afraid.

'Mr Wycliffe . . .'

'One or two points have arisen which I would like to clear up with you and Mrs Innes.'

'Polly is in her studio; I'll fetch her.'

'Not for the moment. If we could talk somewhere in private first . . .'

Innes looked like a man who felt trapped but he made no objection. 'Very well; in here.'

Wycliffe followed him into a small room, obviously his study. The walls were book-lined and there was a desk by the window. On the desk there was a sheaf of lecture notes, heavily annotated in pencil, a carousel from a slide projector, and trays of slides. 'I'm lecturing in Truro on Tuesday to an arts society. One has constantly to revise one's material to present it at different levels . . .'

They sat down. Wycliffe said: 'I've just come from talking to Bertie Harvey, Mr Innes. I know that the two of you have a homosexual relationship. Once I am satisfied that it has nothing to do with either of the crimes under investigation it will be none of my business but, until then . . .'

'*Either* of the crimes, Mr Wycliffe?'

171

'The theft of two paintings by Pissarro, and the murder of Hilda Clemo.'

Innes's long white fingers beat a little tattoo on his desk. After reflection he said: 'I think you should know that my wife does not object to the relationship. It is not a source of emotional conflict between us.'

'Good!'

Innes looked at Wycliffe, perhaps to decide whether he was being ironic.

It was not lost on Wycliffe that Innes had chosen to talk about his homosexual relationship, rather than the paintings or Hilda Clemo.

'As I told you, Polly suffered her injury in a car accident. I did not tell you that I was driving the car at the time and that the accident was my fault.'

'Did this happen before or after your marriage?'

'Before. One might say that our marriage was a direct consequence of the accident.'

'You mean that it was some sort of accommodation?'

'It was natural that Polly should feel she had some claim on me.'

'I see.'

'In the event it has worked well. What is called a normal sexual relationship between us is not practicable or, from my point of view, desirable . . . Anyway, I am what Polly needs and wants, a caring, affectionate companion.'

'What you are telling me is that you were not sexually attracted to Hilda Clemo.'

'I'm saying that I have never been sexually attracted to women.'

'It is your wife who insists on sharing a bed?'

'Polly prefers it that way.'

The window of the little room looked out on a yard and, beyond, to the pine trees, now desolate against the rainswept sky.

'Does your wife go out alone?'

Innes looked surprised by the question but he answered

172

without hesitation. 'Not alone. She spends Sundays with her mother in Truro but I take her there in the morning and bring her back in the evening. Otherwise I am with her when she is away from home.'

'Did Hilda come here on Sundays?'

'She came here on different days. I've already told you, Mr Wycliffe — '

'Please answer the question.'

'All right, she sometimes came on Sunday afternoons; my wife knew this and had not the slightest objection.'

'Where were you on Tuesday night, Mr Innes?'

'Tuesday night?'

'The night Hilda's body was pushed into the quarry pool.'

'I was here — as usual.'

'It seems that your partner was expecting you.'

Innes studied his fingernails. 'I know. We had an arrangement but I couldn't keep it. Polly was upset and I couldn't leave her in the house alone.'

'So you did not leave the house that night?'

'No, I did not!'

When they stopped speaking Wycliffe was conscious of the silence which seemed to close in like some palpable fluid taking possession of a vacuum. He wondered if he had ever known another place where he had been so conscious of the silences as in this strange countryside between the moors and the sea.

Innes sat motionless and pale in the steely-grey light from the window.

'When you went to Exeter on Saturday, where did you stay?'

He seemed to rouse himself from a reverie. 'Near Exeter with a friend who works at the University.'

'What time did you arrive?'

'Half-past seven or a quarter to eight.'

'And you left here at . . .?'

'I told you, at about half-past five.'

'We can check your arrival time.'

'Why should I lie?'

'When Hilda visited you, was she in the habit of walking into the house without knocking?'

A puzzled look. 'We told her to do that.'

'You were talking to her when you were out with the dog at, as you say, "a little before five"?'

'Yes.'

'A witness who knew Hilda says he saw her go into this house at about five o'clock on Saturday afternoon. The door was open and she went in without knocking.'

A longish pause. 'I suppose she might have decided to look in on Polly while I was still out, got as far as the door, then changed her mind.'

'The witness says the dog came out to greet her; he also says that the *deux chevaux* was not in the drive.'

'Then he was mistaken.'

'When you left, where was your wife?'

'I left her working in the studio.'

Chapter Twelve

Friday morning (continued)

Polly Innes listened with all the concentration she could muster, but all she could hear was the rain on the windows. They must have gone into the drawing-room. No! Now he was alone, he would take the policeman into his study. *But what was he saying*? Her hands gripped the arms of her chair so that her knuckles showed white.

She couldn't work; she couldn't think. At first it seemed that she might come to terms with what had happened, there had been hours when she was able to lose herself in her painting. Now she had only to look at the canvas to know that it was useless to try.

She could not keep her eyes off the floor. It was becoming an obsession. Her studio had been built as a garden-room, with windows down one side and a slatted bench for plants. The floor consisted of uneven slabs of blue slate, strewn with rugs. In winter it was warmed by two large oil-stoves, one at each end.

She was still breathing hard from exertion. She had arranged the rugs, and rearranged them. She had reached down from her wheelchair, straining and tugging to get them into a position where they covered the stains — or where the stains had been, or where she thought the stains had been. She had manoeuvred her chair, she had held her head this way and that to catch every angle, every trick of the light. There were no stains.

There was a blank canvas on the easel, already primed; her painting table was laid out — colours, brushes, palette . . . She had set up an arrangement of Michaelmas daisies, grasses and bramble sprays, to be called *Autumn*. Now they were wilting.

'If only I could paint!' Instead she lay back in her chair, exhausted, staring out of the window at the grey emptiness of the sky and she felt vulnerable, flayed . . .

And the cycle was beginning again as it had done through the nights and days. At first it had been a memory, a recollection, but with each repetition it had become more and more of a living experience — vivid and intense.

'Oh, there you are, Polly!'

She had come in, casual, relaxed, with that supreme indolence of youth.

'Where's Tristan?'

She was wearing jeans and a sleeveless shirt with an absurd logo. At her armpit one could see the curve of her breast. Impudent!

'I wanted to see him . . . Sorry! Am I interrupting your work?'

Only words. She made no move to go; she had no intention of going until it suited her.

'There's something I wanted to tell him.'

As usual she stood, looking at the painting on the easel, damning it with her silence. As though she knew . . . As though she knew *anything*!

'I'd forgotten he was going away for the weekend.'

She was lying.

She sat on the little stool — a milking stool they had found in the house when they took it over. 'My stool' she called it. She sat with her back to the easel, staring out of the window, indifferent. Her hair shone like gold, spiralling away from the crown, a vortex; sinuous, gleaming.

'I'm pregnant, Polly.'

She had walked in and taken possession, treating the place as though it was her own.

'I thought he should know — you too. I haven't quite made up my mind what to do about it . . .'

It was like a target, the centre of the gold . . .

176

The blood seeped slowly through the gold — so very slowly. She had taken an age to fall.

'Why are you so anxious to convince me that you were here at the time you believe Hilda was attacked?'

Innes's gaze seemed fixed on the distant pines. 'I've been trying to tell the truth as I recall it.'

'No!'

'I beg your pardon?' A hackneyed response which came mechanically.

'You are lying. You did not meet Hilda on Saturday afternoon; you had already left by the time she reached here on her way home.'

Innes turned slowly to face Wycliffe. 'What could I possibly gain by lying?'

'You may think that you are shielding someone.'

Before Innes could react there was a crash and a muffled cry. Innes was on his feet in an instant and out of the room with Wycliffe at his heels. Innes pushed open a door at the end of a short passage and Wycliffe had a glimpse of a slate floor with rugs, of Polly's wheelchair on its side, and of Polly herself, clear of the chair, crumpled on the floor, one hand clutching at the corner of an orange rug.

Innes said: 'I knew that chair was unstable when she had it made! I've warned her . . .'

They lifted her, a light burden, and carried her along the passage to her bed. Her eyes were open and she followed their every movement but she did not speak.

Innes made consoling noises and asked her questions but did not press for answers.

Wycliffe said: 'I'll call the doctor.'

Innes looked at him but said nothing.

The bedroom was in the front of the house. Wycliffe went to the window from where he could see his parked car and Lucy Lane waiting. It was only a moment or two before she saw him and joined them in the bedroom.

Wycliffe spoke in a low voice. 'She's fallen out of her chair. I want you to stay with her and note down anything she says. Don't leave Innes alone with her in any circumstances.'

He went to his car and contacted the Incident Room on the radio telephone. 'I want Dr Hosking at the Innes place. If he's out on his rounds, find him and get him here. And tell Sergeant Fox that we are ready for him. Also send a WPC for bedside surveillance and I shall need a couple of uniformed men.'

He sat in the car, waiting and brooding. Rain still billowed in from the sea, slanting out of the sky.

The girl.

It was four days since he had first heard of Hilda Clemo and during that time she had seldom been out of his waking thoughts. Now he knew who had struck the blow from which she had died, and he thought he understood the circumstances in which it had been struck. But who had really killed Hilda Clemo? Her death was part of a pattern which she herself had contrived.

One of her teachers had said: 'She can be very cruel.' Her sister, Alice, had said: 'She seems to treat people as though they were white mice or something . . .'

The white-mice image appealed to him; for them you contrive little hoops, ladders, tread-wheels and seesaws, then you sit back and watch their antics. Experimental, rather than cruel, and less emotional. But white mice are less likely to hit back than human beings.

He heard the police vehicles before he saw them, bouncing down the lane; the scenes-of-crime van and an unmarked police car. They pulled into the gravelled space in front of the house, now becoming congested. Fox got out, followed by his assistant; then, from the car, DC Potter, a WPC, and two uniformed PCs.

Fox came over to Wycliffe.

'Tell them to get back into their vehicles and wait, then come back here.'

When Fox joined him again Wycliffe gave him a briefing. 'The probability is that the crime took place in the studio and Franks thinks there must have been a fair amount of bleeding from the head wound. The floor there is of slate slabs with rugs. That's where you start. If you get a positive reaction to the benzidine

178

test, try to get some idea of the extent of the contamination, then hand over to forensic. Dr Drury will be arriving sometime this afternoon. Apart from that I want you to organize a search of the whole premises.'

'Looking for, sir?'

'Where the body was kept for four days, if not in the studio, the clothes the girl was wearing, the weapon — probably a small hammer normally kept in the studio — and anything which may link the premises with the crime. You can get going at once. I want a uniformed man at the gate and another at the house door. No press.'

The doctor arrived at that moment; the red-headed Hosking, in a battered Ford Escort which looked and sounded as though it was kept going by the sheer will power of its owner.

'What is it now?'

'Mrs Innes has turned over her chair.'

'Is she badly hurt?'

'She doesn't seem to be in any pain and she's conscious, but she either can't or won't speak.'

'Why "won't"? Why wouldn't she want to?'

'Perhaps because she is under police supervision.'

The little doctor stopped as they reached the shelter of the doorway and looked up at Wycliffe in astonishment. 'So that's the way the wind blows! What do you want from me?'

'Obviously that she should receive whatever medical attention she needs, in hospital if necessary.'

'And?'

'I want to know if and when in your opinion she is fit to be questioned.'

'All right! Where is she?'

To Wycliffe's surprise Innes did not stay with his wife while the doctor was with her; he joined Wycliffe in the passage. His manner was nervously aggressive. 'I want to know what is happening.'

They moved toward his study and Innes slumped into his chair as though he no longer had the strength to stand on his feet. His face was grey and a tic affected one side of his mouth. Wycliffe remained standing, as though to underline the changed relationship.

'My men are already at work in the studio. They are looking for evidence that Hilda Clemo met her death there, and that her body was kept there, or elsewhere on these premises until the night of Tuesday/Wednesday, when it was taken to and dumped in the quarry pool.'

Innes turned his head as though about to speak but Wycliffe forestalled him. 'In the first place an examination will be made of the studio floor and of the rugs there. Tests will be made for bloodstains and if these are positive, further tests will be carried out to discover whether the blood is human — and so on. It is impossible on a floor like the one in the studio to remove all traces of a spillage of blood.'

'Why are you telling me this?'

'Because I want you to understand that if Hilda Clemo died here we shall find evidence of the fact. I think you have realized all along that once this house became the subject of an investigation, evidence would be found.'

Innes sat, motionless, staring down at his lecture notes which must now seem as relevant as a papyrus scroll; a man in the process of being cut off from his roots. Wycliffe had to remind himself of the photograph that had looked out at him from the case file on Monday morning, and of the pallid, nude body of the girl he had seen being fished out of the quarry pool on Wednesday.

'What do you want me to do?'

'Nothing for the moment. I will talk to you later, officially. In the meantime you can stay here or you can join your wife in the bedroom if you wish. You will not be allowed to leave the house.'

Wycliffe went into the studio where Fox and his assistant were at work. It was his first chance to take a look at the place. It was also the first time he had seen any of Polly Innes's work. There was not a lot of it; just half a dozen canvases propped against a wall. They were all flower studies; slick, professional — raw material for the printmaker; tailor-made for the walls of people who, reasonably, say they know nothing about art but know what they like.

Already Fox had made three or four chalk marks on the slate slabs and over the crevices between them. They were concentrated in an area not far from an easel which now carried a blank, but ready-primed canvas.

'I've made six tests so far, sir, and four of them have given positive results.' As he spoke, his head raised to see through the lower section of his bifocals, he was dripping benzidine sulphate on floor scrapings placed between filter-papers on a glass sheet. A brief pause, before adding a drop or two of hydrogen peroxide, and the result, almost immediately, was a streaky blue/green colouration.

'That's another positive. It seems to me, sir, that she must have lain here for some time after the blow that gave rise to the bleeding — long enough for it to spread some distance from the source.'

Wycliffe had said to Franks: 'So you think she was left to die,' and Franks had replied: 'That's the size of it.'

Time to bring in the experts. The benzidine test was a hoary old stand-by, easy to do, and reliable enough for blood in general, but non-specific. Although it was unlikely that the Inneses had indulged in orgies with rabbit or chicken blood, one had to be sure. In any case the experts would build up a picture in depth and they would be listened to in court if the occasion arose.

Dr Hosking pushed open the studio door. 'A word . . .'

Wycliffe joined him in the passage.

Hosking said: 'She's asking for you.'

'What did you make of her?'

'I don't know. Physically she seems to have done herself no harm, but I suspect that you're going to be lumbered with the trick cyclists. It's possible she's shrewd enough to be aiming for that.'

'Should she be in hospital?'

'Well, you can't put her in a cell, that's for sure; and I don't imagine you want to keep her here. For one thing the consultant gentlemen won't want to come out here, getting mud splashed all over their BMWs.'

'Will you fix it — hospital, I mean? There will have to be a WPC with her for the time at any rate.'

'I'll see what I can do.'

'Is she fit to make a statement?'

'I've told you she's asking for you. I can't say more than that.'

Polly Innes was lying in the middle of the big bed, making a scarcely discernible mound. Her tiny fingers grasped the edge of the bedclothes holding them so that they covered her mouth and nose; only her large dark eyes and her white forehead could be seen. The mass of her hair was spread over the pillow.

The WPC sitting by her got up as Wycliffe came in.

'No, stay where you are.' Wycliffe brought up a chair on the other side of the bed. The eyes watched his every movement.

'You asked to speak to me, Mrs Innes. I must tell you that you do not have to say anything but what you do say may be taken down in writing and given in evidence. Do you understand that?'

The eyes blinked assent.

The WPC looked her question and he nodded. She opened her notebook.

The woman in the bed lowered the bedclothes just enough to free her lips and, after an interval, she said in a surprisingly strong voice, full of venom: 'She hated me, you know! She wanted to take him away just to hurt me . . . She didn't want him; she didn't want anybody. She was ice-cold!' She turned her head to look at the WPC. 'Is she writing this down?'

'Yes.'

That seemed to please her and she turned back to Wycliffe. 'And he's as bad as her. He married me because it was his fault I'm what I am, and he persuaded me that he was homosexual — he said he couldn't cope with a woman . . . Well, I accepted that, I believed him; but as soon as . . . as soon as she came . . .' Her voice was choked by a dry sob.

Wycliffe said: 'I think you would do better, Mrs Innes, to wait until you are asked to make a statement.'

She was gazing at him with a fierce intensity and her voice was forced and harsh. 'I know it's all over for me now, and I don't care, but somebody has got to listen!' She was holding her tightly clenched fists above the bedclothes and they were trembling. 'She came into my studio, asking for him . . . She sat with her back to me . . . "I'm pregnant, Polly . . . I thought he should know — you too. I haven't quite made up my mind what to do about it . . ."

'She was baiting me! That's what she had come for; she knew perfectly well that he was away . . . What she was really saying was: "This is something between Tristan and me. What do you matter? A cripple! There's nothing you can do about anything!" And she wasn't even pregnant! She was lying!'

The outburst relieved some of the tension, the wild look disappeared from her eyes and when she spoke her voice was subdued, reflective. 'So I hit her. I hit her with the little hammer I use for tacking up drapes . . .'

After another long pause she continued in the same quiet strain. 'I hit her . . .' Her right hand made small movements in the air which seemed to suggest the act. 'I didn't kill her. She didn't die for a long time . . . It was horrible! Her eyes wouldn't close and her mouth was open. She made terrible noises and there was blood . . .

'I couldn't stay in the room with her but all through that night I kept coming back and she still wouldn't die . . . I tried to help her.'

'To help her?'

'Yes. I gripped her throat, but I wasn't strong enough . . . I didn't go to bed that night . . .'

The rain had stopped and the skies were clearing. An ambulance arrived to take Polly Innes to the hospital and Innes came out to see her go. There was a strange moment as he stood looking down at her and she up at him. Neither spoke, there was no kiss, not even a touching of hands, they merely gazed at each other as though in mutual disbelief.

When the ambulance had gone Innes returned to his study and in a few minutes Wycliffe, with Lucy Lane, joined him. As they entered Innes turned his head but said nothing.

Wycliffe said: 'This is a formal interview, Mr Innes. I have to tell you that you do not have to say anything but that anything you do say may be taken down in writing and used in evidence.'

Wycliffe placed a chair close to the desk and sat down; Lucy Lane sat near the door, her notebook ready.

'We have evidence to show that Hilda Clemo met her death in this house. We believe that she was attacked by your wife in the studio on Saturday afternoon, after you had left for Exeter. The blow to the back of her skull was not immediately fatal but she was left on the studio floor to die.'

Wycliffe stopped speaking. Innes sat staring out of the window at his pine trees which stood out once more against a sunlit sky. He was quite motionless but a vein in his temple pulsed visibly.

'I think that you returned from your weekend, on Monday, to find Hilda's dead body where she had fallen and where she had lain for two days. How long she took to die is a question that may never be answered. I can understand that you suffered a profound shock. You set about removing the evidence in so far as this was possible but you were faced with the disposal of the body. As I said before, I am sure you realized from the start that your wife's security depended on avoiding any hint of suspicion, for once there was a forensic examination of the studio, evidence was certain to be found.'

The telephone on Innes's desk rang and startled them both. Innes turned, questioning, and Wycliffe nodded. It was some enquiry about a lecture and Innes cut it short. He replaced the telephone with a sigh. 'I'd forgotten there was a world outside.'

Those were the only words he had spoken so far.

Wycliffe was in no hurry to carry on and the silence lasted for a minute, or longer, but Innes gave no sign of impatience or distress. When Wycliffe did resume it was precisely where he had left off.

'There was a limit to how long you could keep the body in the house. It occurred to you that if it was found in the quarry pool — naked — there would be a strong presumption that she had died in consequence of a sexual assault and for that you had a ready-made suspect in Clifford Rule.

184

'But on Tuesday the Rules were taken in for questioning in connection with a separate offence and, though they returned home that evening, it seemed that they might be arrested at any time. So on Tuesday night — or in the early hours of Wednesday — you transported Hilda's body to the quarry and pushed it over the edge.'

Another prolonged silence was broken at last by Wycliffe: 'I have only one more thing to say to you. On Monday evening I came to talk to you and your wife. That afternoon you must have been working frantically to obliterate the gruesome evidence of your wife's crime. Presumably, by that time, you had shifted Hilda's body to somewhere less conspicuous than the studio floor. Yet despite all this you were able to convey an impression of a calm, cultured existence, only slightly ruffled by the unaccountable disappearance of a young girl whom you had taken under your academic wing. In my opinion that would only have been possible to someone devoid of compassion.'

Lucy Lane's notebook had remained blank throughout the interview, now she looked at Wycliffe in astonishment. Never before had she heard him speak of or to anyone in a tone of such contempt.

Innes gave no sign that he had heard; he turned to Wycliffe and asked in a tired voice: 'What happens to me now?'

'You will be taken to the nearest police station, you will be questioned further and given the opportunity to make a fresh statement about the events of Saturday and what followed.'

'Shall I be allowed bail?'

'You haven't been charged yet.'

'But if I am charged.'

'If you are charged you will probably be bailed to appear at a special court hearing tomorrow.'

By arrangement, Wycliffe and Kersey met in The Seiners shortly after one. Wycliffe was subdued, dispirited.

Kersey said: 'What are you going to have?'

'What? Oh, a sandwich and a glass of lager.'

Kersey went to the bar and came back with a plate of

sandwiches and the drinks. Wycliffe was at the little table by the window. The sun was bringing out the tourists and there was a continual passage through the narrow alleyway, to and from the harbour. Wycliffe was watching them as though they were part of a parade of strange animals.

Kersey made an effort to rouse him. 'Try the beef; plenty of horseradish — the real stuff.'

Wycliffe sipped his lager. 'Polly Innes is in hospital with a WPC at her bedside.'

Kersey nodded. 'I gathered that. Has she made a statement?'

'She rambled on in a highly emotional way for a bit but there's been nothing approaching a formal interrogation, and won't be until the medics say she's fit.'

'And Innes?'

Wycliffe was like a man half asleep; he seemed to need time to digest the simplest question or remark. Now he drank a little more of his beer before replying. 'Lucy Lane and Curnow have taken him to the nick for questioning. I don't think they'll have any trouble in getting a statement.'

Kersey pointed to the sandwiches. 'You're not eating.'

'How did the search go?'

'Clean. Not a thing to implicate Harvey in any deal. Certainly no picture.'

Wycliffe nodded. 'I'm not surprised.'

'You think he's already clear of it — or them?'

'No, I think we're probably looking in the wrong places. Anything else?'

'Our frogman has dredged up a pair of wheels from the quarry pool. They look as though they came from some sort of garden trolley but he can't say whether they were there when he was searching for the body.'

Wycliffe picked up a sandwich. Kersey said: 'That's crab.'

'It doesn't matter.'

There was something that Wycliffe was struggling to put into words, more to clarify his own ideas than for Kersey's benefit, but he spoke his thoughts aloud. 'The girl, Hilda — the victim — by deciding to lie about the result of her pregnancy test accomplished her own death; in doing so she created a murderess, and an accomplice to murder.'

Kersey said: 'It's an odd way to look at it but I suppose it's true.'

They were interrupted by a great burst of laughter from the group around the bar, followed by some horseplay in which a glass was broken.

Wycliffe frowned, but carried on with what he was saying. 'She also changed radically the lives and prospects of others about her — her father, Alice, Esther, Harvey, Jane Rule, and Clifford . . . Think of all that our investigation into Hilda's death has uncovered, affecting these people. Doesn't it strike you as odd, how different the world would have seemed to them today if, between leaving the doctor's surgery and arriving home, last Saturday morning, Hilda had not made up her mind to lie?'

Kersey said: 'Pebbles in the pond, colliding ripples and all that, but I don't see where it leads.'

'In court it will be: A killed B in a fit of jealous rage. C was an accessory after the fact. So put A and C in jail. B has already been tidied away.'

'But how can it be otherwise?'

'I don't know, but it seems a simplistic way of dealing with such a web of relationships, don't you think? The classical Chinese had a theory that justice should attempt to restore the pattern.'

'Perhaps we should hand over to the sociologists.'

Wycliffe looked down at the sandwiches and at his half-empty glass. 'I think I'll settle for a coffee.'

Chapter Thirteen

Friday afternoon

At half-past two Wycliffe drove to the Innes place alone. As he turned off the road, past the Moyles', the scene was serenely peaceful under the afternoon sun: the line of blue sea, the pine trees, the grey slate roof of the Innes house and, beyond, the huddle of buildings that was Tregelles. The surface water had not had time to drain away and he bumped over the hidden ruts and potholes. A uniformed policeman stood at the gate and another by the open front door. The *deux chevaux* was flanked by a police patrol car on one side and the scenes-of-crime van on the other.

'Forensic not arrived yet?'

'Not yet, sir.'

'Press?'

'Haven't seen anything of them either, sir.'

Sergeant Fox came to greet him like a tail-wagging dog with his master's slippers. 'I think we've got this one sewn up, sir. It's extraordinary how people, supposed to be intelligent, can be so stupid when they move outside their own line. I've noticed before — '

Wycliffe cut him short. 'You've found something?'

'I'll show you.'

In the studio, spread out on a table, were several tagged polythene bags each containing a single item in the collection: a small claw-hammer, a grey shoulder-bag, and the various items of a girl's clothing.

Fox lifted the bag which contained a navy-blue sweat-shirt with a white logo. 'See that, sir? The back is caked with blood.'

Wycliffe, troubled, was curt: 'All right! Where did you find all this?'

'You'd scarcely believe it, sir, but the hammer was in that cupboard over there, with other tools; the clothing and the bag were tucked away under bedding in a chest of drawers.'

The contents of the shoulder-bag were displayed separately: a purse, with about five pounds in coins; a small packet of tissues; a few tablets of phenacetin in a tube, and a ball-point pen.

'No engagement book, diary . . . nothing of that sort?'

'No, sir.' Fox added: 'I'm expecting Dr Drury from Forensic at any minute, sir. I suppose you will be here?'

'I may not be. If I'm not, tell him I shall be back shortly.'

Wycliffe was in a strange mood; a mood in which relief was mingled with a consciousness of failure — perhaps not so much failure as inadequacy. Although he had just now been complaining to Kersey about what he called the ABC routine — the linear argument — really that was what criminal investigation was about, it was what he was paid for, to disentangle from the web that single strand which led from victim to culprit. He had tried to take in the whole pattern without success and the pattern was still incomplete.

He left the bungalow on foot and picked his way down the muddy lane towards the farm. With mild surprise he saw that nothing had changed. The hens still pecked between the cobbles and the rabbits still scuffled and thumped in their hutches. He realized with a slight shock that it was little more than twenty-four hours since his last visit.

The door was open and he called: 'Anybody at home?'

Jane Rule came to the door, a wooden spoon in her hand. 'Oh! You better come in.'

The kitchen was pervaded by the smell of stewing black-berries. A preserving pan simmered on the stove.

'Clifford picked some blackberries so I'm putting 'em down for jam.' She stirred the pan with her spoon then turned to face him again. 'Anyway, what do you want now?'

'So they finished the inventory.'

'They finished yesterday evening.'

189

'I know; and they didn't find the picture — the picture that was hanging over Agnes Rule's bed, the one you liked, which Hilda sketched, and Bertie Harvey was called in to inspect.'

She was looking at him with her grey expressionless eyes. 'I don't know what they found; they didn't tell me.'

'Where is it?'

'I don't know what you mean.'

Wycliffe did not raise his voice but there was no mistaking his mood. 'Mrs Rule, I can have men here within a few minutes. If I have to call them they will search every inch of space in this house; it won't be just another inventory. When they have finished in the house they will start on the outside buildings, and they will carry on until they find what they are looking for. When they do, you will be open to a charge — '

She had turned away, and was shifting the pan off the heat. 'I don't want it to boil . . . You better come upstairs.'

He followed her up the stairs to Agnes's bedroom.

'It's behind there.' She pointed to one of the paintings, a heavily varnished rustic scene: *Farmyard with cows and two figures*. 'I thought it would be safer.'

'Safer from whom?'

She shrugged her shoulders.

He lifted the heavy frame off the wall and turned it over on the floor. The Pissarro, still on its stretcher but without the frame, was protected by a sheet of polythene and secured behind the other canvas by a strip of lath, wedged into place. Wycliffe removed the painting and laid it on the bed, reflecting that never before had he handled an art treasure. At close quarters, without a frame, and lying on the bed obliquely lit, it was hard to take it seriously.

'I haven't done anybody any wrong. The frame is under the bed.'

'Does Harvey know the picture is here?'

She looked at him as though the question was a foolish one.

'You thought that even if Clemo laid claim to the stuff in the old dairy he wouldn't feel that he could take away what was actually in the house.'

The grey eyes met his, a blank stare.

'And after a while you could try your hand at finding a buyer.'

Saturday afternoon

The major part of the investigation was over. For days to come men would be engaged in supplementary enquiries; there would be weeks of paperwork and many hours spent with police lawyers thrashing out the case to be sent to the Public Prosecutor. But now Wycliffe was at home in his garden. It was hot, and he was sitting on a slatted seat under a cherry tree, sipping an ice-cold drink. The voices of his wife and daughter came to him from somewhere down amongst the rhododendrons. Macavity, the Wycliffe cat, was stalking birds which he would never catch.

James Clemo, Bertie Harvey, Jane Rule, Clifford, Tristan Innes, Polly Innes . . . and Hilda Clemo: all caught in a tangled web to which they had each contributed something. And it had been his job to sort it out.

He looked at his watch; it was five o'clock. One week ago Hilda Clemo had walked up to the Innes front door, the dog had come to greet her, and she had gone in without knocking . . .